Friedrich Glauser was born in Vienna in 1896. Often referred to as the Swiss Simenon, he died aged forty-two, a few days before he was due to be married. Diagnosed a schizophrenic, addicted to morphine and opium, he spent much of his life in psychiatric wards, insane asylums and, when he was arrested for forging prescriptions, in prison. He also spent two years with the Foreign Legion in North Africa, after which he worked as a coal miner and a hospital orderly. His Sergeant Studer crime novels have ensured his place as a cult figure in Europe. *Thumbprint* has been made into a film and has been translated into six languages. This is its first publication in English.

Germany's most prestigious crime fiction award is called the Glauser prize.

THUMBPRINT

Friedrich Glauser

Translated from the German by
Mike Mitchell

BITTER LEMON PRESS
LONDON

BITTER LEMON PRESS

First published in the United Kingdom in 2004 by
Bitter Lemon Press, 37 Arundel Gardens, London W11 2LW

www.bitterlemonpress.com

First published in German as *Schlumpf Erwin Mord (Wachtmeister Studer)* by Limmat Verlag, Zurich, 1995

Originally published as *Wachtmeister Studer* in
Zürcher Illustrierte in 1936

This edition has been translated with the financial assistance of
Pro Helvetia, the Arts Council of Switzerland

© Limmat Verlag, 1995
English translation © Mike Mitchell, 2004

A CIP record for this book is available from the British Library

ISBN 1–904738–00–1

Typeset by RefineCatch Limited, Bungay, Suffolk
Printed and bound by WS Bookwell, Finland

Contents

A man has decided to call it a day

The prison warder with the triple chin and red nose muttered something about "never a moment's peace" when Studer dragged him away from his lunch. But Studer was from the Criminal Investigation Department of the cantonal police, only a lowly sergeant, true, but Liechti couldn't simply tell him to push off.

So the warder got up, filled his tumbler with red wine, drained it, picked up his bunch of keys and went with Studer to the cell where Schlumpf, the prisoner the sergeant had delivered hardly an hour ago, was locked up.

Corridors . . . long dark corridors . . . the walls were thick. Thun Castle felt as if it had been built to last for ever. The winter cold was still lurking everywhere. It was hard to imagine that outside was a lake bathed in a warm May day, people strolling in the sun, others on the water in their boats, rocked by the waves, getting a tan.

The cell door opened. Studer paused for a moment on the threshold. The window was high up, with two horizontal and two vertical bars crossing it. The ridge of a roof could be seen, with old black tiles, and above it the brilliant blue of the sky.

But there was a man hanging from the lower cross-bar! A leather belt had been tied in a tight knot round it. The dark shape of a body slanted across the white-washed wall, its feet resting on the bed at a strangely twisted angle. And the buckle on the hanged man's neck shone where the sun caught it from above.

1

"Christ Almighty!" said Studer, shot forward, jumped up onto the bed — the warder was amazed at the nimbleness of a man already middle aged — and grasped the body in his right arm while his left hand was undoing the knot.

Studer let out an oath — a broken fingernail — then climbed down and gently laid the lifeless body on the bed.

"If you bloody lot weren't so far behind the times here," said Studer, "and at least had wire mesh over your windows, this kind of thing wouldn't happen. There we are. Come on Liechti, get a move on and fetch the doctor."

"All right, all right," said the warder, a note of anxiety in his voice, and hobbled off.

Studer immediately started artificial respiration. It was a reflex action. From the days when he had taken a first-aid course. It was only after he had been doing this for five minutes that it occurred to him to place his ear on the man's chest to see if his heart was still beating. Yes, it was. Slowly. It sounded like the ticking of a clock someone had forgotten to wind up. Studer continued to pump the man's arms up and down. Underneath his chin a red line ran round his neck, from ear to ear.

"Oh you fool, Schlumpfli," Studer said softly. He took out his handkerchief, mopped the sweat off his own brow then wiped the man's face. A boy's face, young, two deep furrows over the bridge of his nose. Defiant. And very pale.

So this was Erwin Schlumpf. The man he'd arrested that morning in a hamlet in the Upper Aargau. Arrested on suspicion of the murder of Wendelin Witschi, merchant and travelling salesman from Gerzenstein.

Pure chance that he'd arrived in time! About an hour ago he'd delivered Schlumpf to the prison. It had all been done according to regulations, the warder with the triple chin had signed for him and there was nothing to stop Studer getting the train back to Bern and forgetting the whole thing. It wasn't the first arrest he'd made and it wouldn't be the last, either. Why had he felt the urge to go and see Erwin Schlumpf again? Chance?

Perhaps . . . What was chance anyway? . . . He did care what happened to this Erwin Schlumpf, that much was true. In fact he had quickly come to like Erwin Schlumpf . . . Why? . . . Standing there in the cell, Studer stroked the back of his neck with the flat of his hand a few times. Why? Because he had never had a son of his own? Because the man had kept on protesting his innocence during the journey here? No. They were all innocent. But Schlumpf's protestations had sounded genuine. Although . . .

Although it was an open-and-shut case. Wendelin Witschi, travelling salesman, had been found on Wednesday morning, lying on his front in a wood not far from Gerzenstein with a bullet hole behind his right ear. His pockets were empty, but the murdered man's wife claimed her husband had had three hundred francs on him.

And on Wednesday evening Schlumpf had paid for a few drinks in the Bear with a hundred-franc note. The local policeman from the rural gendarmerie had gone to arrest him the next morning, but Schlumpf had already fled.

So that was how it came about that on Thursday evening the police captain had come to see Sergeant Studer in his office and said, "Studer, you need some fresh air. Go and arrest this Erwin Schlumpf tomorrow morning. It'll do you good. You're getting too fat. . ." Which was true, unfortunately. Usually a uniform

3

corporal was sufficient for such an arrest. This time it just happened to be the detective sergeant. Was that chance? . . . Fate?

Whatever it was, he had become involved with Schlumpf and he had come to like him. A fact! And facts one had to accept, even if they were only facts about feelings.

Schlumpf! Not a pillar of society, certainly. Known to the cantonal police. Illegitimate. The authorities had had almost constant dealings with him. His file at the welfare office must weigh a good three pounds. The story of his life? Put into service with a farmer as a boy. Stole things. — Perhaps the little lad was hungry? How can you be sure afterwards? — Then things followed the course they always do in this kind of case. Tessenberg Reform School. Ran away. More stealing. Caught. Beaten. Finally released. Burglary. Witzwil Labour Camp. Released. Burglary. Thorberg Prison, three years. Released. And then nothing. For two whole years. Schlumpf had got a job in Ellenberger's tree nursery in Gerzenstein. Sixty rappen an hour. Fell in love. They wanted to get married. Get married! Studer snorted. A lad like that getting married! And then came the murder of Wendelin Witschi . . .

It was well known that old Ellenberger liked to employ ex-convicts in his tree nursery. Not just because they were cheap labour, no, Ellenberger seemed actually to enjoy their company. Well, we've all got our little quirks and it was undeniable that persistent offenders tended to keep on the straight and narrow at old Ellenberger's . . .

And now, just because he'd paid with a hundred-franc note in the Bear on Wednesday evening, Schlumpf was supposed to have murdered a man?

4

What was the lad's explanation? It was his savings. He carried them round with him . . .

Chabis! he thought. What rubbish! Savings? At sixty rappen an hour? That made a hundred and fifty francs a month, give or take a few rappen. His room? Thirty. Food? . . . Two francs fifty a day was a minimum for a man doing heavy work. Seventy-five plus thirty, that made a hundred and five, five for laundry . . . cigarettes, the pub, the dance hall, the barber's, the baths . . . at best he'd have five francs a month left. And from that he'd managed to save three hundred francs in two years? Impossible. And carrying the money round with him? Psychologically inconceivable. People like that couldn't carry money round without it burning a hole in their pockets. In the bank? Perhaps. But in his wallet??

But Schlumpf had had three hundred francs on him. Almost, anyway. Two hundred-franc notes and around eighty in change. Studer checked the list of prisoner's possessions he had signed when he handed Schlumpf over: "Wallet, contents: 282 Fr. 25."

So it all fitted. Even his attempt to escape at the railway station in Bern. A stupid attempt. Childish. Yet so understandable. It would be a life sentence this time . . .

Studer shook his head. And yet. And yet . . . There was something not quite right about the whole business. For the moment it was just an impression, a gut feeling. Studer shivered. It was cold in the cell. It was about time that doctor came. And how long was Schlumpf going to take to wake up?

The man's chest rose in a deep breath, his eyeballs returned to their normal position and Schlumpf was staring at the policeman. Studer started back. An uncomfortable stare. And then Schlumpf opened his

5

mouth and screamed. A hoarse scream: fright, fear, an attempt to ward off the horror . . . There was a lot in that cry. It seemed never-ending.

"Quiet. Will you be quiet," Studer whispered. His heart started to race. Finally he did the only thing possible and placed his hand over the screaming mouth.

"If you're quiet," he said, "I'll stay with you for a while and you can have a cigarette after the doctor's gone, eh? I came just in time . . ." He attempted a smile.

But Schlumpf did not return the smile. The look in his eyes did become less wild, but when Studer took his hand away Schlumpf said quietly, "Why didn't you leave me hanging there, sergeant?"

Not an easy question to answer. After all, he wasn't a priest . . .

It was quiet in the cell. The sparrows were chirping outside. In the yard below a little girl was singing a folk song in a thin, reedy voice:

> My angel art thou,
> My rosemary bough,
> I will be faithful for ever and ay . . .

Then Studer said, and his voice sounded hoarse, "Hey, didn't you tell me you were going to get married? The lassie . . . she'll stick by you, won't she? And if you say you're innocent then it's not at all certain you'll be found guilty. Trying to kill yourself is the most stupid thing you could have done, don't you realize that? People will see it as an admission of guilt . . ."

"I wasn't just trying, I really wanted to."

But Studer didn't need to respond. Steps could be heard in the corridor and Liechti's voice saying, "He's in there, Herr Doktor."

"Up again, are we?" the doctor asked, taking Schlumpf s wrist. "Artificial respiration? Splendid."

Studer got up off the bed and leant against the wall.

"Well, then," the doctor said, "what shall we do with him? At risk. Suicidal. Not the first one we've seen. We'll have to request a psychiatric report ... won't we?"

"I don't want to be sent to the lunatic asylum, doctor," Schlumpf said, loud and clear. Then he coughed.

"You don't? And why not? Yes, well, we could ... Liechti, you must have a double cell where you could put the man. So that he's not all on his own? ... You have? Splendid." Then softly, in a stage whisper, every word clearly audible, "What has he done?"

"The murder in Gerzenstein," the warder whispered back, just as clearly.

"Oh, oh," the doctor nodded. A worried nod, or at least so it seemed. Schlumpf turned his head and looked across at Studer. Studer smiled, Schlumpf smiled back. They understood each other.

"And who is this gentleman?" the doctor asked, embarrassed by the smiles Studer and Schlumpf had exchanged.

Studer stepped forward so briskly the doctor drew back. The policeman stood there, stiff. His pale face with its remarkably narrow nose didn't quite seem to go with the slightly overweight body.

"Sergeant Studer of the cantonal police." It sounded pig-headed, provocative.

"Really. Delighted to meet you, delighted. And you're in charge of the investigation?" The blond-haired doctor was trying to regain his composure.

"I arrested him," said Studer curtly. "And I'd be quite happy to stay with him for a while until he's calmed down. I've plenty of time. The next train back to Bern doesn't go till half past four."

"Splendid," said the doctor. "Marvellous. You do that, sergeant. And this evening you'll put the prisoner in a two-man cell. Won't you Liechti?"

"Yes, Herr Doktor."

"Good day to you, one and all," said the doctor, putting on his hat. Liechti asked if he should lock the door. Studer waved the suggestion away. Open doors were probably the best antidote to prison psychosis.

Their steps echoed down the corridor.

Studer took his time over pulling the straw out of his Brissago, lighting it and holding it under the end of the cheap cigar. He waited until the smoke came billowing out, then stuck it between his lips.

Then he produced a packet of Parisiennes from his pocket. "Go on, take one." Schlumpf drew the smoke from his first pull at the cigarette deep into his lungs. His eyes shone. Studer sat down on the bed.

"You're a good man, Sergeant," said Schlumpf.

Studer had to take hold of himself to suppress a funny feeling in his throat. He got rid of it by having a good yawn. "Right Schlumpfli," he said. "Now. Why did you want to end it all?"

It wasn't easy to explain, Schlumpf replied. Everything had been ruined. And he knew how the whole business worked. Once you were arrested you were stuck. With his criminal record! And this would be enough for a life sentence ... And the girl the sergeant had spoken of, she wouldn't want to wait. She'd be bloody stupid if she did.

"Who is the girl?"

"Sonja. She's the daughter of Witschi, the man who was murdered."

"And does Sonja think you committed the murder?"

8

That he couldn't say. He'd just run off as soon as he'd heard they were accusing him of it.

How had suspicion come to fall on him?

Because of the hundred-franc note he'd paid with in the Lion, of course.

"In the Lion? Not in the Bear?"

"It could have been the Bear. Yes, of course it was the Bear! The Lion's for the nobs. We played there once on some occasion or other . . ."

"Played? Who? What kind of occasion?"

"A wedding. Buchegger played the clarinet, Schreier the piano, Bertel the double bass. And I played the accordion."

"Schreier? Buchegger? But . . ." Studer frowned. "Don't I know them?"

"I should think so," said Schlumpf and a faint smile appeared at the corners of his mouth. "Buchegger talks about you a lot. So does Schreier. You collared him three years ago . . ."

Studer laughed. "Aha. Old friends. And you've got together to form a folk band?"

"Folk band?" Schlumpf looked insulted. "No. A real jazz band. Ellenberger, our boss, even gave us an English name. The Convict Band."

Schlumpf seemed quite happy to talk about minor matters, but when the conversation came round to the murder he immediately tried to change the subject.

Studer was content to let him. Schlumpf could ramble on as much as he liked if he got pleasure out of it. Don't push. Everything comes in its own good time if you've enough patience.

"Then you'll have played in the villages round about?"

"You bet."

"And earned a fair bit?"

"A tidy sum . . ." Hesitation. Silence.

"In that case, Schlumpfli, I'm quite prepared to believe you didn't kill Witschi — in order to steal his wallet. You had three hundred francs saved up?"

"Yes, three hundred . . ." Schlumpf looked up at the window and sighed. Perhaps because the sky was so blue.

"So you were going to marry the daughter of the murder victim? She's called Sonja? And her parents, were they happy with the idea?"

"Her father was. Old Witschi — the 'murder victim' as you put it — said he had no objections. He often came to see Ellenberger and he used to talk to me as well. He told me I was a decent lad and even if I did have a record, well, judge not etc. I wouldn't get up to anything stupid once I was married to Sonja, he said. Sonja was a good girl . . . And then the boss had promised to make me head gardener, Cottereau being pretty old and me being a good worker . . ."

"Cottereau? The one who found the body?"

"Yes. He goes for a walk every morning. The boss lets him do as he pleases. Cottereau comes from the Jura but he's been here so long you wouldn't notice he's a Frog. Wednesday morning he came running back to the nursery and told us Witschi was in the woods, dead, he'd been shot. The boss sent him to report to the gendarmerie station."

"And what did you do when you heard the news from Cottereau?"

Ach, they'd all been worried, said Schlumpf, because suspicion was bound to fall on them, having criminal records. But it was quiet all day, no one had come to the nursery. Only Cottereau found it difficult to calm down, until the boss told him pretty sharply to put a stop to his whining and moaning.

10

"And on Wednesday evening you paid with a hundred-franc note in the Bear?"

"Wednesday evening, yes . . ."

Silence. Studer had left the yellow packet of cigarettes lying on the bed beside him. Without asking, Schlumpf took one. Studer gave him the packet and a box of matches. "Hide them. But don't let anyone catch you."

Schlumpf gave a smile of thanks.

"When do you knock off in the evening at the nursery?"

"Six o'clock. We have a ten-hour day." Then he added, suddenly animated, "This gardening work is something I know about. The supervisor at the reform school in Tessenberg said I was good at it. And I don't mind hard work . . ."

"I'm not interested in that." Studer deliberately adopted a harsh tone. "So after you knocked off you went back to the village, to your room. Where were you living?"

"With the Hofmanns, in Bahnhofstrasse. You'll easily find the house. Frau Hofmann was nice . . . They're basket-weavers."

"Just stick to the point. You went to your room and had a wash? Then you went out for your dinner? Is that right?"

"Yes."

"So: you knocked off at six." Studer took a notebook out of his pocket and started to write everything down. "Six o'clock: finished work; half past six, a quarter to seven: dinner." He looked up at Schlumpf. "Did you eat quickly? Slowly? Were you hungry?"

"Not very."

"You ate quickly and were finished by seven . . ."

11

Studer seemed to be concentrating on his note-book, but his eyes were not still. He saw the change in Schlumpf's expression and asked a harmless question to relax the tension. "How much did your dinner cost?"

"One fifty. I always got a soup for lunch at Ellenberger's, and I used to take some bread and cheese with me. He charged us fifty rappen for a plate of soup and gave us an afternoon snack for nothing, Ellenberger always treated us proper, we like him, he has this funny way of talking and he looks a hundred years old, no teeth left, but . . ." All this in one breath, as if Schlumpf was afraid of being interrupted, but this time Studer simply ignored his effusion.

"What were you doing on Wednesday evening between seven and eight o'clock?" he asked sternly. Holding his pencil at the ready between his slim fingers, he didn't look up.

"Between six and seven?" Schlumpf was breathing heavily.

"No, between seven and eight. You finished your dinner at seven and at eight you were in the Bear paying with a hundred-franc note. Who gave you the three hundred francs?"

Studer looked the young man straight in the eye. Schlumpf turned away, then suddenly threw himself over on one side and buried his head in the crook of his arm. His whole body was trembling.

Studer waited. Not dissatisfied with the course the interview had taken. He wrote "Sonja Witschi" in small letters in his notebook and put a large question mark after it. When he went on, his voice had softened.

"We'll sort all this out, Schlumpfli. I deliberately didn't ask you what you were doing on Tuesday evening, before the murder. You would have just lied to me.

I'm sure it'll be in the files and, anyway, I can ask your landlady. But tell me one thing. What kind of a girl is Sonja? Is she an only child?"

Schlumpf's head shot up. "There's a brother. Armin."

"And you don't like Armin?"

He'd given him a proper thrashing once, said Schlumpf, baring his teeth like a snarling dog.

"Armin didn't like the idea of you going round with his sister?"

"No. And he was always having rows with his father. Witschi used to complain about him often enough . . ."

"Aha . . . And the mother?"

"The old woman's always reading novels . . ." ("The old woman", the lad said. No respect there.) "She's related to Aeschbacher, the mayor, he got her the kiosk at Gerzenstein station. She spent all her time sitting there, reading, while Sonja's father went round hawking his goods. Well, not exactly hawking. He was a travelling salesman. He went round on his motorbike, a Zehnder, selling floor polish, coffee, that kind of thing. And they found his Zehnder not far away. Parked beside the road . . ."

"And where was Witschi's body?"

"A hundred yards away, in the woods, Cottereau said . . ."

Studer was doodling in his notebook. Suddenly he was miles away. He was in the hamlet in the Aargau where he'd arrested Schlumpf. His mother had opened the door. A strange woman, Schlumpf's mother. She hadn't been at all surprised. She'd just asked, "But he can have his breakfast first, can't he?"

A young girl in Gerzenstein, an old mother in the Upper Aargau . . . and between them a young lad, Erwin Schlumpf, accused of murder . . .

It all depended on what the examining magistrate who handled the case was like. He ought to have a word with the man. Perhaps . . .

Steps could be heard approaching. The warder appeared in the doorway, a gleam of malice on his red face. "Sergeant, the magistrate would like a word with you."

And Liechti grinned. An insolent grin. It wasn't difficult to guess what it meant. A simple policeman had exceeded his authority and was being invited to receive the rocket he so justly deserved.

"Goodbye, Schlumpfli," said Studer. "Don't do anything stupid. Should I say hello to Sonja for you if I see her? Yes? Right then. I might perhaps come and see you. Goodbye."

As Studer walked down the long corridors of the castle, he couldn't get the look with which Schlumpf had watched him go out of his mind. Nor could he tell what it meant. There was astonishment in it, yes, but was there not also a despair beyond hope lurking beneath it?

A silk shirt, a signet ring and gold-tipped cigarettes

"You are . . ." He cleared his throat. "You are Sergeant Studer?"

"Yes."

"Sit down."

The examining magistrate was small, thin, yellow. His jacket was a purplish brown and had thick shoulder pads. To go with his white silk shirt he had a cornflower-blue tie. There was a coat of arms engraved on his broad signet ring, a ring which looked old.

"Sergeant Studer, I would like to ask you, in all politeness, what you think you are doing? Could you explain how you came to involve yourself without authorization — I repeat, without authorization — in a case which . . ."

The examining magistrate broke off, though he couldn't have said why himself. The man on the chair before him was a detective, a simple policeman. He was middle-aged and there was nothing special about him: a shirt with a soft collar, a grey suit that had gone slightly baggy in places because the body inside it was fat. He had a thin, pale face with a moustache covering his mouth so that you didn't know whether he was smiling or not. And this simple policeman was sitting there in the chair, legs apart, forearms resting on his thighs, hands clasped . . .

The magistrate himself couldn't have said why he suddenly adopted a slightly warmer tone.

"You must realize, Sergeant, that it looks to me as if you've exceeded your authority." Studer nodded and nodded. Of course, his authority! "You had handed over this Erwin Schlumpf to the prison officer, all according to regulation. What reason did you have for going back to see him again? Your return, I have to admit, was highly opportune, but that is not to say that it is covered by police authority. You have been with the force long enough, Sergeant, to know that productive collaboration between the various branches of the legal system is only possible if each ensures it stays strictly within the limits of its own authority . . ."

That word: authority. Not just once, no, three times. Now Studer knew where he stood. That's a piece of luck, he thought, they're not the worst, the ones who keep going on about their "authority". You just have to be nice to them and let them see you take them seriously and you have them eating out of your hand in no time at all . . .

"Of course, sir," said Studer, his voice exuding meekness and respect, "I am well aware, all too well aware that I have exceeded my authority. As you have quite rightly pointed out, I should have delivered the suspect to the prison and left it at that. But then — the flesh is weak, sir, the flesh is weak — then I thought the case was perhaps not such an open-and-shut one as I had at first assumed. It was just possible, I thought, that further investigation might be necessary and I might end up in charge of it, so I thought I might as well put myself in the picture . . ."

The investigating magistrate was visibly mollified already. "But the case is clear, Sergeant," he said. "And after all, even if this Schlumpf had hanged himself, it would have been no great loss — I would have been relieved of an unpleasant case and the state wouldn't have to bear the cost of a trial."

"True, sir. But if Schlumpf had died would that really have solved the case? I'm sure you too will soon work out that Schlumpf is innocent."

Really, such a statement was a piece of insolence. But Studer's voice was so respectful, so compelling in its plea for approval, that all the gentleman with the signet ring could do was nod agreement.

The walls were panelled in brown wood and the air, since the shutters outside the windows were closed, gleamed like dull gold.

"The file on the case," said the examining magistrate a little uncertainly, "I haven't had time to look at the file yet. Just a moment . . ."

To his right there were five files piled on top of each other. He picked them up in turn. The last one, the one at the bottom, the thinnest, was the right one. On the blue cardboard cover was written:

Schlumpf, Erwin:
MURDER

"Unfortunately," said Studer, putting on an innocent face, "unfortunately there have recently been quite a number of reports of investigations not being carried out as thoroughly as they might. That suggests it would be advisable, even in such a clear-cut case, to proceed with due caution . . ."

He couldn't repress a mental grin. "Authority" — "proceed with due caution": two could play at that game.

The magistrate nodded. He took a pair of horn-rimmed spectacles out of their case and put them on. Now he looked like a melancholy film comic.

"Certainly, certainly, Sergeant. But you must bear in mind that this is my first serious investigation, so of course your experience in these matters . . ."

He broke off. Studer made a dismissive wave of the hand.

But the examining magistrate ignored it. He took out two photographs and handed them to him across the table.

"Photographs of the scene of the crime," he said.

Studer examined the pictures. They weren't bad, even though they had obviously not been taken by someone trained in forensic photography. Both showed the undergrowth of pine woods and on the ground, which was covered in pine needles — the pictures were very sharp — a dark figure lying on its front. On the right-hand side of the back of the bald head, a couple of inches or so from the ear and just above the fringe of thin hair, which partly covered the jacket collar, was a dark hole. It didn't look very pleasant, but Studer was accustomed to that kind of picture. His only question was, "The pockets empty?"

"Just a moment. I have Corporal Murmann's report here . . ."

"Aha," Studer broke in, "so Murmann's in Gerzenstein, is he?"

"You know him?"

"Yes, yes, a colleague. A long time since I last saw him, though. So what's Murmann written?"

The magistrate turned the sheet of paper over and started muttering words and phrases to himself. ". . . male corpse . . . lying on its front . . . bullet-hole behind right ear . . . bullet lodged in head . . . probably from a 6.5 Browning . . ."

"He knows about weapons, does Murmann," Studer remarked.

"Pockets empty," the magistrate concluded.

18

"What?" said Studer quite sharply. "Do you happen to have a magnifying glass?" The polite deference had completely vanished from Studer's voice.

"A magnifying glass? Yes. Just a moment. Here you are."

For a while all was quiet. A ray of sunlight fell through a gap in the shutters right on Studer's hair. In silence the magistrate examined the figure sitting before him, his broad, rounded back, his hair, shining like the coat of a dapple-grey horse.

"That's funny," said Studer in a soft voice. (What the devil's funny about a picture of a murdered man, the magistrate wondered.) "The back of his jacket's quite clean . . ."

"The back's clean? Well, what of that?"

"And the pockets were empty," was all Studer said, as if that explained everything.

"I don't understand . . ." The magistrate took off his glasses and cleaned the lenses with his handkerchief.

"If you visualize the man here," — Studer tapped the photograph with the magnifying glass — "the man here being ambushed and shot from behind, then the position of the corpse suggests he fell forwards onto his face. Doesn't it? He ends up lying on his front and doesn't move any more. But his pockets were empty. When were they emptied?"

"The attacker could have forced Witschi to hand over his wallet . . ."

"Not very likely. What does the post-mortem have to say about the probable time of death?"

The magistrate leafed through the papers with the keenness of a schoolboy desperate to get a good mark from his teacher. Remarkable how quickly the roles had reversed. Studer was still sitting on the uncomfortable chair, which was presumably normally kept for prisoners who were being interrogated, and yet it looked as if he was the one who had taken charge of the matter.

"The post-mortem examination," said the magistrate, cleared his throat, adjusted his glasses and started to read: "Occipital bone smashed . . . the mesencephalon . . . lodged close to the left . . . But you don't want to hear all that . . . Here . . . Death occurred approximately ten hours before the body was found . . . That's what you wanted to know, sergeant? The body was discovered between half past seven and a quarter to eight in the morning by Jean Cottereau, the head gardener at Ellenberger's tree nursery . . . That means the murder must have taken place at around ten o'clock the previous evening."

"Ten o'clock? Good. How do you visualize it? Old Witschi's coming back from his rounds, puttering along quietly on his Zehnderli. Suddenly he's stopped . . . Already there's a lot that's not clear. Why did he get off? Was he afraid? . . . Let's assume someone stopped him. Right, he's forced to lean his bike against a tree and go into the woods . . . Why doesn't his assailant just take the wallet there on the road and make off with it? . . . But he doesn't. He forces Witschi to go a hundred yards — it was a hundred yards, wasn't it? — into the woods. Shoots him from behind. Witschi falls on his front. Can you tell me, sir, at what point the wallet with the three hundred francs that has disappeared was taken out of his pocket?"

"Wallet? Three hundred francs? Just a moment, Sergeant, I need to have a look at the report."

Silence. The buzzing of a fly reverberated through the room. Studer had hardly moved, kept his head lowered.

"You're right. Frau Witschi states that in the morning

her husband told her he would probably be bringing a hundred and fifty francs home with him that evening. Some accounts were due. And he took a hundred and fifty francs with him, she said . . . Enquiries by telephone have established that two of Witschi's customers did indeed pay their bills. One of a hundred francs, one of fifty . . ."

"One of a hundred and another of fifty? Strange . . ."

"Why strange?"

"Because Schlumpf had three hundred-franc notes on him. One that he used to pay at the Bear and two I took off him. What happened to the wallet?"

"You're right, Sergeant, this case does have some obscure factors."

"Obscure factors!" Studer shrugged his shoulders. An awkward customer, thought the magistrate. He was as nervous as when he took his *Staatsexamen*. Perhaps the sergeant was susceptible to flattery . . . "I can see that your training in criminological practice is superior to my own, sergeant," he said.

Studer muttered something.

"What did you say?" The magistrate put his hand behind his ear, as if he didn't want to lose a single word Studer said.

But Studer suddenly seemed to have forgotten where he was. He went through the elaborate ceremony of lighting one of his cheap cigars.

"Wouldn't you prefer a cigarette?" the magistrate asked timidly. He hated the smell of Brissagos. He held out an open cigarette case across the desk. Studer shook his head. Offering him, Studer, a simple policeman, cigarettes with a gold tip!

The magistrate broke the silence with a question. "Where did you acquire your practical skills, Herr Studer?"

But not even the change in the form of address —
Herr Studer instead of sergeant! — could rouse the
silent policeman from his rumination.

"How is it that with all your experience and skills you
haven't even made it to police lieutenant?"

Studer's head shot up. "What? . . . How do you
mean? . . . Is there an ash-tray?"

The magistrate smiled as he pushed a brass bowl
across the table.

"I worked with Professor Gross in Graz. Why I
haven't got on? Well, if you must know, I got my fingers
burnt in a case involving a bank. I was an inspector
with the Bern city police at the time . . . Yes, and during
the war . . . After the business with the bank I was in
disgrace and had to start from the bottom again. These
things happen . . . But what I was going to say, how do
you intend to deal with this matter? What steps will you
take?"

At first the examining magistrate felt like putting the
man in his place, making it clear to him that he was the
one who gave the orders, after all, it was he who bore
the responsibility for the investigation. But then he
dismissed the urge. There was something so anxiously
expectant about Studer's look. So he said, in a conciliatory tone, "Well, the usual ones, I imagine. Summon
the Witschis for interview, and the boss of the . . . the
. . . accused . . ."

"Erwin Schlumpf," Studer broke in. "Previous convictions for burglary, theft and other minor offences."

"Correct. Basically, then, the type of character one
could believe well capable of the crime, don't you agree?"

"It's certainly . . . possible." Pause. "But even a man
with a record's not a magician. And Schlumpf'll keep
his mouth shut, however long you go on interrogating
him. He'll let them send him to Thorberg for life —

and once he's there he'll string himself up again. It's a shame about the lad, really, yes, a real shame . . ."

"All due respect for your feelings of humanity, Herr Studer, but we have an investigation to carry out, haven't we?"

"Yes, of course. By the way, is the body still in Gerzenstein?"

Again the magistrate leafed through the file. "It was transferred to the Institute for Forensic Medicine on Wednesday evening. Von Roggwil, the commissioner of police, gave the order personally . . ."

Studer counted off on his fingers: "On Wednesday May 3 at half past seven in the morning the body is found. The first autopsy around midday by Dr . . . Dr . . . What was his name now?"

"Dr Neuenschwander."

"Neuenschwander. Good. Wednesday evening Schlumpf uses a hundred-franc note in the Bear. Thursday he runs away. Today, Friday, I arrest him at his mother's. When was the body taken to the Institute?"

"Wednesday evening . . ."

"And when do you think we can expect the report from them?"

"I thought we might confront the accused with the body. What do you think?" The question was put politely, but the thought going through the examining magistrate's mind was: I wish the fellow would shove off soon, that Brissago stinks and he's pushy, I'll make an official complaint, but what's the point? That won't get rid of him any quicker. We'll just have to be nice to him . . .

"Confront him?" Studer repeated. "To get him to make another attempt to escape?"

"What? He tried to get away from you? And you didn't tell me?"

Studer looked at the magistrate calmly. He shrugged his shoulders. What answer was there to a question like that?

"I'll be quite open with you, sir," he suddenly said in a voice that sounded strangely husky and agitated. "We've been beating about the bush for long enough. I know what you'll be thinking. This old detective, been demoted, not long to go till he retires, he's a bit full of his own importance. And he's being pushy. I'll get someone to give him a good dressing-down. This very evening, as soon as he's gone, I'll telephone police headquarters and complain . . ."

Silence. The magistrate had a pencil in his hand and was drawing circles on his blotting pad. Studer got up, grasped the back of the chair, swung it round so that it was in front of him, leant his elbows on the back-rest — the Brissago between his fingers gave off a cloud of smoke — and said, "I'll tell you something, sir. I'll be quite happy to hand in my resignation if the investigation is not carried out in the way I would wish. But if I do resign, then I can do as I like. That should be fun. I promised Schlumpf I'd take the matter in hand . . ."

"Have you become an advocate, Sergeant?" the magistrate interjected in a mocking tone.

"No. But I could employ one. One who'd demolish the prosecution case — during the trial. If that's what you'd prefer? But you'd better imagine how it'll be first. You'll be called as a witness for the defence, and then all the mistakes in the preliminary investigation will be held against you. Would you like that?"

The fellow's completely mad! the magistrate thought. A real troublemaker. Why did they have to send this Studer of all people to carry out the arrest. With a mania for justice. I thought they'd died out ages ago! I've gone along with everything he's said . . . Is the

24

man a mind-reader? What a mess! If this Schlumpf does turn out to be innocent, then there could well be a public outcry, there'll be accusations of . . . Better to go along with the fellow. Out loud he said:

"What's the point in all this, Sergeant? I don't know much about the case. And threats? There's no need for these strong-arm tactics. Have I refused to listen to you? You're impatient, Herr Studer. Let's discuss this matter calmly. It's seems to me you're rather touchy, Sergeant, but you must remember that other people can get irritated too."

The magistrate waited, and while he waited he stared at the Brissago between Studer's fingers.

"Oh, I see," Studer suddenly said. "So that's it." He went over to the window, pushed open the shutters and threw his cigar out. "I should have thought. Your kind of people . . . Was that the reason? I felt you had something against me and I thought it was because of Schlumpf. And it was only my Brissago?" Studer laughed.

An odd fellow, the magistrate thought. Understands quite a lot . . . The stench of his Brissago. Can something like that trigger off a hostile reaction?

While these thoughts were going through his mind, Studer said, "Funny, isn't it, how some trivial habit in another person can get on our nerves. Smoking a cheap cigar, for example. With me it's expensive gold-tipped cigarettes." And with that he sat down again.

"Aha," was all the magistrate said. But inside he was full of admiration for Studer's mind-reading. Then he added, "I think I will have this Schlumpf — your protégé — brought up for interview now. Would you like to be present?"

"Very much so. But . . . do you think you could . . ."

"Yes, of course." The magistrate smiled. "I'll treat him so that he doesn't go and hang himself again. Not for the moment, at least. I can do it both ways, you know. And I'll speak with the public prosecutor. If a further investigation should prove necessary, we'll ask for *you*."

Billiards and chronic alcoholism

Studer played his shot. The white ball rolled across the green baize, hit the red, bounced off the cush and missed the other white ball by a whisker.

Studer placed the butt of his cue on the floor, screwed up his eyes and said, "Needed a touch more side spin."

And that was the moment at which he first heard the booming voice he was to hear many more times. It was saying:

"And believe me, they're barking up the wrong tree in this Witschi business; there's something not quite right there, you can believe me. Arresting Schlumpf . . ." That was all Studer managed to hear. The silence, which had hung over the room for a moment, burst and the babble of voices started up again. Studer turned round and had a good look at the man with the distinctive booming voice.

He was tall, with a thin, furrowed face. Sitting next to him at a small table in the corner was a short, fat man who kept nodding, nodding while the skinny old man went on talking, leaning on his elbows and wagging his finger. His lips were almost invisible, the man couldn't have any teeth at all. His hand came down, picked up his glass without looking, put it to his lips then suddenly realized it was empty. The hard mouth cracked into a gentle smile, the smile of a man who doesn't take himself entirely seriously.

"Rösi," he said to the waitress who was passing his table, "Rösi, two more beers."

"Yes, Herr Ellenberger." The red-haired waitress did not withdraw her hand when he patted it. She looked like a cat who wanted to purr, but was looking for a spot where she could do it in peace.

"*Your* shot . . ." said Studer's opponent, Münch, the lawyer. He wore a high, stiff collar.

While Studer was lining up the balls, eyes screwed up, he kept thinking, Ellenberger? Ellenberger? Talking about the Witschi business? And while he was wondering whether it could be the same Ellenberger who had a tree nursery in Gerzenstein, the Ellenberger who was Schlumpf 's employer, he naturally messed up his shot. He hadn't chalked his cue properly and the tip skidded off the ball with a scraping noise that set his teeth on edge.

The cloth on the table, with the bright light shining down on it, gave off a green glow, turning the gently billowing smoke a bizarre colour. A laugh that sounded like a croak came from Ellenberger's table, but it wasn't the old man laughing, it was his fat companion. And in the silence that followed, Studer heard Ellenberger say, "Yes, Witschi, he wasn't stupid. But Aeschbacher now, a day-old calf's less . . ."

"What is it, Studer?" Munch asked. No reply.

This Witschi business was starting to get on his nerves. Studer had thought he could forget about it for this evening at least. Then you go to your local for a game of billiards and who should be sitting there but Ellenberger, talking in a loud voice about Witschi. And it's goodbye to your quiet evening . . .

The photograph of the murdered man's back . . . A back on which there were no pine needles . . . The bullet hole in the back of his head . . . The odd Christian names the family had . . . Wendelin, the father was called, the daughter Sonja, the son Armin. And the mother? Anastasia perhaps? . . . Why not?

Witschi . . . it sounded like the chirping of sparrows. Wendelin Witschi, a travelling salesman puttering along on his Zehnder who was found shot in the woods . . . And Frau Witschi, who sat in the station kiosk reading novels . . .

And while Studer stood there, leaning on his cue watching Münch play — he really did seem to be in form this evening — he heard the pleasantly booming voice again: "What'll our Schlumpf be doing? What d'you think, Cottereau? I suppose the plods'll have nabbed him by now?"

The word "plods" gave Studer a start. He was inured to the mockery the police were exposed to. Just that one blasted word with its dull, thudding sound had the power to drive him wild. People who used it sounded so superior, so self-satisfied, he'd once said to his wife. And when he heard it now, coming from Ellenberger, he automatically swung round and stared at the man.

He found himself looking into a pair of eyes that were fixed on him, eyes that made him feel uncomfortable. He couldn't keep it up for long. They were strange, Ellenberger's eyes. They gave an impression of coldness, the pupils were almost vertical slits, like a cat's. And the iris a bluish green, very light.

"Another game?" Munch asked. He had made his break in silence and now he was finished.

Studer shook his head.

"D'you know that man over there?" he asked pointing over his shoulder with his thumb. Münch craned his neck in his high collar. "The old man there? Sitting with the little tubby one? I should think so. That's Ellenberger. He came to consult me today. Regarding a certain Witschi. You've heard of him, haven't you? The Witschi who was murdered a couple of days ago? He owed Ellenberger money. I saw Witschi once, too . . ."

Münch paused and started to make calming gestures with his right hand, which looked like a seal's flipper. When Studer turned round he saw that Ellenberger was waving the lawyer over.

Münch crossed the room. When he reached the little round table, he shook hands with Ellenberger, then waved Studer over. The policeman was introduced, at which it became clear that both he and Ellenberger had heard of each other. The back of Ellenberger's hand was covered with blotches the colour of withered beech leaves.

"Did you feel insulted when I said plods just now, Sergeant? I saw you twitch like a young stallion when it hears the crack of the whip."

"Oh that," said Studer, "that's just the same as gardeners not liking being called clodhoppers. Am I right?"

Ellenberger laughed, a deep bass laugh, fluttered his crinkled eyelids and sucked in his lips between his empty gums, but said nothing. For quite a while his expression remained fixed. The effect was grotesque, antediluvian.

They sat down at the little table where wasn't really enough room. Next to them was an open window. It was muggy; outside, a hot wind was drifting past, and the sky was smeared with a sickly grey paste.

Without having to be asked, the waitress placed four tall glasses of beer on the table.

"*Gesundheit*," said Studer, raised his glass, tipped it to his lips and put it down again. His moustache had a line of white foam stuck to it. "Aah . . ."

With his thumb and forefinger Ellenberger made his glass perform a slow dance on the beer-mat. Then he suddenly asked, "Have you heard anything about Schlumpf?"

He'd arrested him that morning, Studer said quietly Where?

At his mother's.

Silence. Old Ellenberger shook his head, as if he wasn't clear about something.

The things the pl— the police had to do, he said, weren't always very nice. Going to fetch a son from his mother! For his part, he preferred grafting roses, even digging over the ground in winter.

Münch drummed his fingers on the table, twisting and craning his neck in embarrassment. The short fat man, who was called Cottereau and was therefore the head gardener who had found the body, blew his nose on a large red handkerchief.

Studer let the silence hang over the table and looked past Ellenberger out of the window.

"And? How is Schlumpf?" the latter asked angrily.

"Oh," said Studer calmly, "he strung himself up."

The lawyer spluttered audibly and stared at his friend in astonishment, but Ellenberger jumped up, rested his fists on the table and asked in a loud voice, "What did you say? What did you say?"

"Yes," Studer repeated placidly, "he strung himself up. You seem to take a great interest in the lad?"

"Puh!" Ellenberger swept Studer's question aside. "I didn't mind having him around. He kept his nose clean while he was working for me. And now he's dead . . . Hmmm . . . That's the second one the old witch has on her conscience, she and her . . . and her . . ." Ellenberger broke off. "So he's dead?" he asked.

"That's not what I said," Studer replied, scrutinizing his Brissago. "I arrived just in time to . . . to save him. At least that's how you might put it, though . . ."

"So he's not dead? And where is he now?"

"In Thun," said Studer pleasantly, his eyes disappearing beneath his eyelids. "In Thun, in clink. I've talked to the examining magistrate," he went on, "he's open to argument, the case isn't hopeless, but murky, very murky. That's the big problem. And the court likes nice clear cases, they provide the best trials . . . But Schlumpf's denying everything, that makes things difficult, the case'll come up before a jury, of course. And with juries you never know . . ." All this interrupted by long pulls, alternately at his beer and his Brissago.

"But," he went on, "you broke off just now. You were saying something about an old witch. Who did you mean? Frau Witschi?"

Ellenberger avoided the question. "If you want to know something, sergeant, you'll have to come to Gerzenstein. Have a look at the place. It'll be worth your while . . ." Then, with a sigh, "Yes, he had a hard time of it, did Witschi. Often used to complain to me, the old soak. But lots of people booze. Never get married, sergeant."

He was already married, Studer said, and couldn't complain. "So Witschi used to booze?"

"Yes," said Ellenberger, "and so much that Aeschbacher, the mayor — the man looks like a pig with scarlet fever — wanted to get him locked away in the labour camp at St Johannsen."

After a while Ellenberger asked, "Did Erwin mention me?"

Yes, Studer replied, Schlumpf had spoken well of his boss. Since when, he asked Ellenberger, had he joined the welfare service for released prisoners?

"Welfare?" He didn't give a shit for welfare, he needed cheap labour, *voilà tout.* As for treating the lads decently, that was all part of business, otherwise they'd simply clear off again. He'd knocked about a bit, he had, and respectable people made him sick, but the black sheep, as they put it, provided some variety. Overnight you could be mixed up in some criminal case, be connected with a murder, *par exemple,* and that was fun.

He stood up. "I must be off home, Sergeant — come on Cottereau — I imagine we'll meet again. Drop in if you're in Gerzenstein. Goodbye . . ."

Ellenberger waved the waitress over, said, "The lot," and gave her a juicy tip. Then he headed for the door. The last details Studer noticed about the old man were bizarre enough: to go with his poorly cut linen suit he was wearing a pair of brown shoes, not the boots you would expect. And the socks peeping out from underneath the too-short trousers were made of black silk . . .

*   *   *

The next morning Sergeant Studer wrote his report. His office smelt of dust, floor polish and stale cigar smoke. The windows were closed. Outside it was raining, the few warm days had been a snare and a delusion. A harsh wind was blowing through the streets and Studer was in a bad mood. How was he to write this report? Or rather, what should he put in, what leave out?

He heard his name called from the doorway.

"What's up?"

"The examining magistrate from Thun has been on the phone. You're to go to Gerzenstein . . . You arrested that Schlumpf yesterday. How did it go?"

Schlumpf had made an attempt to give him the slip at the station, Studer said, but got nowhere with it. He stayed sitting at his desk, looking up at the police captain.

"Well in that case," said the captain, "leave your report. You can do that later. Go now. It would be best if you went to see Forensic first. Perhaps they'll be able to tell you something."

He'd intended to do that in any case, Studer muttered grumpily, got up, took his macintosh, went over to his little mirror and brushed his moustache. Then he went to the hospital.

The assistant pathologist who came to meet him was wearing a tie with a wonderful pattern of red and black checks, tied in a tiny little knot under his stiff collar. When he spoke he placed the fingers of one hand flat on the ball of the other and subjected his fingernails to a critical, slightly disgusted scrutiny.

"Witschi?" the assistant asked. "When did he arrive?"

"Wednesday, Wednesday evening, Doctor," Studer replied in his best German, with hardly a trace of his native Swiss.

"Wednesday? Wait, Wednesday, you say? Ah, now I know, the alcoholic corpse."

"Alcoholic corpse?" asked Studer.

"Yes, imagine, a blood-alcohol level of 210. The man must have been drinking before he was shot. I tell you, Inspector . . ."

"Sergeant," Studer stated baldly.

"We will say inspector here, sounds better. You must understand, please, it was not simply the concentration of alcohol in the blood but the condition of the organs. I tell you, Inspector, I never see such a beautiful cirrhosis of the liver, never. Fantastic, I tell you. Has the man never been in a lunatic asylum? No? Never seen white mice or a cinematograph on the wall? Little men, who are dancing, you know? No? A regular delirium tremens? He never has? Oh, you do not know. Pity. And he was shot! At a distance of three feet, I estimate, no traces of powder on the skin, therefore I say three feet. You understand?"

While he was listening to this torrent of words, Studer's mind was occupied with a completely irrelevant question: to which nationality did the young man with the minuscule tie-knot belong? Finally, with the last "You understand", he had the answer.

"*Parla italiano?*" he asked in a friendly voice.

"*Ma sicuro!*" The euphoric outburst was unstoppable and, with a smile, Studer let the words wash over him. The assistant pathologist was so delighted he took Studer affectionately by the arm and led him inside. The professor wasn't there yet, he said, they could talk undisturbed and he, the assistant, knew just as much about the matter as the professor. He had performed the autopsy himself.

Studer asked whether it was still possible to see Witschi. It was still possible. The body had been preserved. Soon Studer was standing by the corpse.

So this was Wendelin Witschi, born in 1882, therefore fifty years old: head almost completely bald, as yellow as old ivory; an apology for a moustache, sparse, drooping; a soft, flabby double chin. The most remarkable thing about it, though, was the calm expression on the face.

Calm, yes. Now, in death. But the face was much wrinkled . . . Good that the man was released from his troubles . . .

But what it was not was the face of an old soak, and Studer said, "He doesn't really look like a common-or-garden alcoholic . . ."

"Common-or-garden alcoholic! What a wonderful expression!"

The two started to talk shop, Witschi's body still between them. The way he was lying there, the bullet hole behind his ear was not visible. And while Studer and the Italian were discussing an insurance fraud which had caused quite a stir in the specialist press (a man had shot himself and made the suicide look like murder), Studer suddenly asked, pointing at the corpse, "Something like that wouldn't be a possibility in this case, would it?"

"Out of the question," said the Italian, who had in the meantime introduced himself as Dr Malapelle from Milan. "Completely, absolutely impossible. To cause a wound like that, he must hold his arm so . . ." And he demonstrated the position with his elbow pushed back towards his shoulder blade as far as it would go. He used his fountain pen in place of a revolver. The tip of the pen was only about four inches away from the spot behind his right ear where the corpse had the bullet hole.

"Out of the question," he repeated. "There would have been traces of powder. Because there were no traces, we conclude the distance must have been more than three feet."

"Hm," said Studer. He wasn't entirely convinced. He turned back the sheet covering the dead man. Witschi had remarkably long arms . . .

"Resignation!" Studer suddenly said out loud, as if a word he had long been searching for had just occurred to him. It described the dead man's expression.

"*Fatalismo*! Precisely. He knew it was all over. But I do not know whether he know he is going to die."

"Yes," Studer conceded, "it could be he was expecting something else. But something he could do nothing about."

Felicitas Rose and a Parker Duofold

The girl was reading a novel by Felicitas Rose. At one point she held the book high enough for Studer to see the illustration on the cover: a man in jodhpurs and shiny riding boots was leaning against a balustrade, with swans swimming on a castle moat in the background; a young woman dressed all in white was coyly playing with her parasol.

"Why do you read rubbish like that?" Studer asked. Some people have an allergy to iodine or bromine, Studer's allergy was to Felicitas Rose and other romantic novelists in the style of Hedwig Courths-Mahler. Perhaps because his wife used to read that kind of story, all through the night sometimes, which meant that his morning coffee was weak and lukewarm, and his wife had a soulful expression on her face. And a soulful expression across the breakfast table . . .

At his question the girl looked up, went red and said angrily, "That's none of your business." She tried to continue reading but seemed to have lost the taste for it. She shut the book and stowed it in a grubby briefcase which, as Studer observed, also contained two dirty handkerchiefs, a fountain pen of imposing proportions and a handbag.

Studer put on a friendly smile and observed her closely. He had time . . .

The train was crawling through a landscape of grey. Raindrops made dotted lines on the glass, then dribbled down to form murky little puddles at the bottom of the window. Then more raindrops dotted the window . . . hills appeared . . . a forest shrouded in mist . . .

The girl had a pointed chin, freckles on the bridge of her nose and at her temples, which were very white. The high heels of her shoes were worn on the inside. Whenever her shoe slipped down it revealed a hole in her dark stocking, at the back, on the heel.

The girl had produced a season ticket for the conductor. She must make this journey frequently. Where was she going? Gerzenstein perhaps? Her hair was done in a little bun and she had a beret pulled down over her right ear. The blue beret was dusty.

When the girl happened to glance his way, Studer gave her a benign, fatherly smile, but benign-and-fatherly cut no ice. The girl stared out of the window.

Her hands twitched restlessly. Her fingernails were dirty. There was an inky mark on the inside of her right index finger.

The girl opened her briefcase again, rummaged round inside and eventually found what she was looking for.

It was a fat, genuine Parker Duofold, a brown, decidedly masculine pen.

The girl unscrewed the top, tried the pen out on her thumbnail, then took the novel out of her briefcase again, though not to read it. The last page was to be used for writing practice. She scribbled. Studer stared at the letters as they appeared one by one:

"Sonja." Then the nib formed more letters: "With my everlasting love, Sonja."

Studer looked away. If the girl were to glance up now she would certainly be either embarrassed or angry. There was no point in making people embarrassed or angry for no good reason. You had to do that often enough anyway when you were a detective.

The conductor walked past. When he reached the door to the next carriage, he turned round and called out, "Gerzenstein."

The girl kept the Parker Duofold in her hand, dropped Felicitas Rose and the handsome count in polished riding boots into her briefcase and stood up.

A shed with a transformer. Lots of detached houses. Then a bigger house. With a sign: "Gerzensteiner Advertiser. Emil Aeschbacher Printer." In the garden beside the house was a wire-mesh cage. Little brightly coloured budgerigars were perched on the bars, frozen stiff.

A squeal of brakes. Studer stood up, grasped his suitcase and went to the door. His blue raincoat filled the gangway.

It was still drizzling. The station-master had put on his heavy overcoat, his red cap was the only spot of colour in all the grey. Studer went over to him and asked where the Bear Inn was.

"Up Bahnhofstrasse then left, the first large building with a garden beside it." The station-master walked off and left him.

Where had the girl got to? The girl who had written in small, slightly shaky writing on the back page of a paperback novel, "With my everlasting love, Sonja." Sonja? There weren't many girls called Sonja . . .

There was the girl, standing at the kiosk, the windows of which were papered over with colourful book and magazine covers. She was bending down at the little sliding window and Studer heard her say, "I'm going home now, Mother. When will you be coming?"

The reply was inaudible.

So it was Sonja Witschi. He'd better have a look at the mother as well. The mother who had got the station kiosk through the good offices of the mayor, Herr Emil Aeschbacher.

Frau Witschi had the same pointed nose, the same pointed chin as her daughter.

Studer bought two Brissagos from her then sauntered across the station square. An arc lamp. Round the base a flowerbed with stiff red tulips. A wireless was blasting out the Deutschmeister March from one of the upstairs windows of the station building. The girl, Sonja, was walking along about fifty paces in front of Studer.

A pale young man in a white coat with blue lapels was standing outside a barber's. Sonja went up to him. Studer stopped to look in a shop window, watching the couple out of the corner of his eye. They held a whispered conversation, then the girl handed the young man some object and trotted off. From the shop came the sound of a throaty voice saying, "And now follows the time signal from the Chronometrical Observatory in Neuchâtel . . ." And from the shop outside which Studer was standing, though muffled by the closed door, came the march, Sambre et Meuse.

"Gerzenstein is certainly a village that loves its music," Studer said to himself as he went into the barber's.

He put his case down, hung his blue raincoat on the coat stand and sat down in the chair with a sigh.

"Shave," he said.

As the young man bent over him, Studer saw, sticking out of his top waistcoat pocket between the blue lapels of his barber's coat, the fat fountain pen Sonja had taken from her briefcase in the train.

Studer tried a random shot. "Not bad, eh, when you've got a girlfriend who gives you an expensive fountain pen for a present?"

For a moment the lather-covered brush hovered over his cheek. Studer observed the hand holding it. It was trembling. So there was something going on. But what? Studer looked at the young man's sallow complexion in the mirror. His too-red lips were drawn back, revealing his top teeth, which were a brownish colour and decayed. Had Sonja fallen in love with this pasty-faced specimen? Schlumpf was made of finer stuff, despite his past, despite his despair yesterday . . . Yesterday? Was that only yesterday? A man hanging from the window bars, a man screaming in a cell where the winter cold still lurked, while outside a little girl sang, "I will be faithful for ever and ay."

The brush had resumed its gentle progress round Studer's cheeks.

Had he given him a shock, Studer asked the pasty-faced youth. The barber's assistant shook his head. There was nothing wrong, Studer went on in reassuring tones, with getting a present from your girlfriend. Though he did find it strange that a girl who had holes in her stockings could make a gift of such an expensive fountain pen . . .

She had inherited the pen from her father. Yes, inherited it. The young man's voice was hoarse, as if his mouth, tongue and throat were completely dry.

The wireless in the corner was blaring away. Suddenly Studer sat up and listened. What the man at the microphone somewhere far away was saying concerned him. The barber's assistant, who had been absentmindedly stirring the brush round in the bowl, stopped even that activity and stood stock-still.

The distant voice had a note of urgency:

"Before we continue our concert, I have a short announcement from cantonal police headquarters in Bern. Herr Jean Cottereau, head gardener at the

Ellenberger tree nursery in Gerzenstein, has been missing since yesterday evening. It appears to be a particularly brutal case of abduction, although the motive is as yet unknown. Yesterday evening the missing man returned from Bern with his employer, Herr Gottlieb Ellenberger, by the ten o'clock train. As they were about to turn off the road onto a farm track outside the village of Gerzenstein, they were both knocked down by a car that came up behind them without lights. Herr Ellenberger hit his head on the kerb and suffered mild concussion. When he came to his companion, Herr Cottereau, had disappeared. Nor was there any trace of the vehicle. Despite a violent headache, Herr Ellenberger went straight to the local police station. The search of the village and surroundings, organized by Corporal Murmann of the rural gendarmerie and carried out with the help of some of the local inhabitants, produced no results. So far no trace of the missing man has been found. The following description has been issued by the cantonal police:

Height: 5 foot 3 inches, build: corpulent, complexion: red, balding, wearing a black suit . . . Anyone with information should contact . . ."

The young man took a few shuffling steps. A click. The voice fell silent. Then he came back. The sound of a razor being stropped could be clearly heard.

"Razor OK?" the barber asked after he had shaved one cheek. Studer muttered something.

Silence again.

The shave was finished. Studer washed off the soap in the basin.

"Stone?" the youth asked, rhythmically squeezing the rubber bulb of a powder puffer.

"No," said Studer, "powder."

Otherwise nothing was said.

As he left, Studer noticed a pile of cheap paperback novels on a table at the back of the shop. He looked at the title of the one on top. *The Memoirs of John Kling* it said. And underneath: *The Mystery of the Red Bat.*

There was a grin underneath Studer's moustache as he left the shop.

Shops, wireless sets and a village policeman

"Gerzenstein!" Studer muttered. Every house had a sign attached to it, on both sides of the street: Butcher, Baker, Grocer, a branch of the Coop, of Migros; an inn among them, then another: The Merry Monk, The Grapes. Then more: Butcher, Chemist, Tobacconist; a large sign: Chapel of the Apostolic Community. Beyond it, in a garden: Salvation Army. A strip of meadow interrupted the sequence. But immediately after it continued: Chemist, Pharmacy, Baker. A doctor's nameplate: Eduard Neuenschwander MD. Oh yes, the man who'd made the first, superficial examination of the body. Then, finally, — Studer was already beginning to think he'd gone the wrong way — a broad, imposing building of grey stone with a projecting roof: the Bear Inn.

Sergeant Studer asked for a room and was given one with a sloping ceiling and a dormer window. It was clean and smelt of wood. The window looked out onto a meadow at the back covered in a froth of white flowers. Beyond the meadow was the delicate violet of a field of rye and, bordering the view, the woods with a few light green patches of deciduous trees in front of the black of the pines. It was a combination that pleased Studer greatly. He stood at the window for a few minutes, then unpacked his case, washed his hands and went back downstairs. Telling the waitress he would be back for lunch in about half an hour, he set off to look for the local police station.

And as he walked along the village street, past all the signs, like pictures in an exhibition, he noticed a second peculiarity of Gerzenstein. There was music coming from every house, sometimes unpleasantly loud from an open window, sometimes more muffled, if the windows were closed.

"Gerzenstein, village of shops and wireless sets," Studer muttered and felt as if with those words he had characterized part of the atmosphere of the village.

Corporal Murmann of the rural gendarmerie looked like a retired champion wrestler. His uniform jacket was unbuttoned and his shirt gaped open too, revealing a chest on which the hair grew thicker and more profusely than on his head.

"*Salut*," said Studer.

"Studer! Well I never! Still playing billiards?" Telling him to take a seat, Murmann raised his voice in a thunderous roar ending in a long-drawn-out "ee" sound. The call was directed at Frau Murmann. What wasn't clear was whether she was called Emmy or Anni, but what did it matter after all?

"White or red?" Murmann asked.

"Beer," was Studer's brief reply.

The thunderous roar arose again, and two "ee" sounds echoed though the house. This time there was a reply, and the reply was just as thunderous. Only one note higher. Then Frau Murmann appeared in the doorway. She looked like a statue of Helvetia from the 1880s, only her face was much, much more intelligent than the said statue's. Of course, intelligence is not a requirement of patriotic images. What would be the point?

Did she remember Studer, the ex-champion wrestler wanted to know, and the intelligent Helvetia nodded. She had big hands and her handshake was powerful.

Then she asked whether Studer had already eaten. He'd ordered lunch in the Bear, Studer replied, at which the large couple got angry. It wasn't right, it went without saying that Studer would eat with them; the booming duet brooked no refusal. Fortunately for Studer, a third voice started squawking on the upper floor, at which Frau Murmann — Anni or Emmy? — left. Studer had to promise faithfully to come to dinner that evening.

"Yes, hmmm," said Studer, emptied his glass, sighed, "Aaah," and sat there in silence.

"Yes," said Murmann, emptied his glass, burped, got tears in his eyes from the fizz, and then he too fell silent.

It was peaceful in the little office. In one corner stood an old typewriter. The keys gleamed yellow, but it was large and solid and went with Corporal Murmann. Through the window, which was open, Studer could see out into a garden: there were low boxwood hedges round the beds, in which the spinach had already shot up. But in the middle of the garden, where the boxwood hedges formed twisting arabesques, were lustrous red tulips. Their modest entourage of yellow pansies was already fading. They reminded him of people who did not belong to any political party and so had not got anywhere in life.

"You're here because of Witschi," Murmann said, lowering his thunderous voice. The squawking upstairs had stopped and Murmann didn't want to set it off again.

"Yes," said Studer, stretching out his legs. It was a comfortable chair, it had armrests. Studer relaxed and looked through half-closed eyes out into the garden, where the sun was shining. But the brightness didn't last, the grey returned. Only the tulips continued to glow.

Studer thought back to his interview with the examining magistrate. The way he'd had to sweat blood! Murmann was definitely preferable, even if he wasn't wearing a wild-silk shirt.

It was so quiet here, Studer said after a while. Murmann gave a laugh. He hadn't got a wireless like all the other Gerzensteiners, he said. At that Studer laughed too.

Then they both fell silent again.

Until Studer asked Murmann whether he thought Schlumpf was guilty.

"*Chabis!*" was all Murmann said.

But that one word gave Sergeant Studer greater confidence in his own gut feeling that the lad was innocent than all his subtle criminological and psychological observations.

Studer knew that Murmann was a man of few words. Getting him to talk was not easy. The words we throw around in our banal, everyday conversations, yes, he was ready enough with those. But as soon as it was a matter of more important things, a homely Swiss idiom like *Chabis* — cabbage, i.e. nonsense — was worth almost as much as the logical deductions of an expert witness.

"You don't know this dump Gerzenstein," Murmann said after a while. He had filled a pipe and was smoking it slowly.

"I've been here six years now," he went on. "And I know my way around. I can't do anything. I have to watch my step. You know, diplomacy. (At that, for Murmann, rather grand word, he slowly closed one eye.) " It's good that you've come. My hands, you know ..." He stretched out his arms in front of him, his powerful wrists held close together to show how powerless he was.

Then he fell silent again.

"You know," he said after a while, "Aeschbacher, the mayor . . ." Another long silence. "But old Ellenberger!" The right eye winked at Studer.

"But Cottereau's disappeared," Studer interjected, and took a draught of his beer.

"Don't fret yourself," said Murmann placidly. "He'll be back."

"Errr . . . but wasn't it you who informed police headquarters and got them to announce it over the radio?"

"Me?" Murmann asked, his huge, hairy index finger pointing at his chest. "Me? Are you off your head, asking a stupid question like that." It was Ellenberger who'd done it, he went on, just for the hell of it. Beromünster, he'd once heard Ellenberger say, hadn't been set up for nothing. You had to give those people at Swiss Radio something to do. And with all these wireless sets around . . .

A remarkable village, this Gerzenstein, Studer thought to himself, and the villagers even more remarkable, but he decided he had pestered Corporal Murmann for long enough. Anyway, by now his lunch must be waiting for him in the Bear. So he took his leave, promising to return in the evening. Murmann seemed to appreciate his consideration, for as he said goodbye he added that there would be plenty of time for talking then, he always felt sleepy during the middle of the day. If you had to do the rounds of all the inns every evening at closing time, then your head tended to go round and round all day as well. He had a good yawn as he spoke.

So Studer was back in the street. On either side, as far as the eye could see: shops, shops and more shops.

And the houses were not silent.

It was Saturday afternoon.

Through the walls, through the windows, open and closed, came the yodelling of Gritli Wenger, yodelling in their Sunday . . .

Another man who wants to call
it a day

The bacon joint was tough and the sauerkraut floating in too much liquid. The inn was empty. At the bar
the waitress was polishing glasses. It had finally
stopped raining, but the sky was covered with a layer of
dazzling white.

Studer felt an unpleasant stinging in his nose. Presumably a cold coming on. Hardly surprising when
May was so chilly. He had a sip of the coffee. It was as
weak and lukewarm as his wife's after she'd been up
all night reading one of her romantic novels. Studer
poured his kirsch into the watery brew, ordered
another and started to look through the *Gerzensteiner
Advertiser*. His mood slowly improved and he leant
back in the corner, shifting his shoulders until they felt
comfortable against the wall.

A young man came in. With a brusque movement of
her hand the waitress cut off a male voice that was
quietly rambling on about the decisions which the par-
liament had been plagued with during the last week
(there was a click). After that she said, "Hi." It sounded
like a suppressed exclamation of joy and Studer
pricked up his ears, just as even the most stolidly
respectable man will whenever romance raises its
bashful head in his vicinity.

"A lager," the young man said curtly. It was a clear
rebuff.

"Yes, Armin," said the waitress meekly, if a little
reproachfully.

Armin? Studer had a better look at the lad. He was one of those young men who have a thick head of hair and pile it up over their forehead in permanent waves. His blue jacket was so tightly cut at the waist that it had horizontal creases, his wide, lightcoloured trousers hung down over his heels and almost dragged along the ground.

His face? Yes, there was a certain similarity to another face Studer had seen that morning in the harsh brightness of the mortuary. The lad's face was thinner, smoother, and he had no moustache, but there was the same weak, slightly chubby chin.

Another stroke of luck. That must be Armin Witschi. Perhaps his guess would be confirmed.

The waitress came close up to the lad. Armin tolerated it. Didn't he have to look after the shop? she asked.

His sister had come home, he replied, she was free this afternoon and didn't have to go back to Bern. Anyway, he went on, he was fed up with everything. No one came to the shop any more, soon he'd have to start travelling round like his father, and perhaps ... The pause he left was intended to sound meaningful.

"Armin, no!" said the waitress. She was probably about thirty.

Her not unattractive face was marked by weariness.

On no account must he become a travelling salesman, she protested. Schlumpf wasn't the only one, there were others working at Ellenberger's who would stop at nothing ...

She suddenly realized Studer was listening and lowered her voice to a whisper. Armin took a sip of his beer. When he drank he stuck his little finger out.

The waitress's whispering became more urgent. Armin only threw in the odd word, but these few words carried weight, more weight than they deserved, Studer was tempted to say. He took out his pocket watch. Half past two. He was tired, his muscles were aching, the whispering was getting on his nerves. Perhaps he should go for a little walk? To Ellenberger's? To see his old friend Schreier, who was playing the piano now, and Buchegger with his double bass? The jazz band with the English name, The Convict Band! Had a sense of humour, did old Ellenberger. You never knew quite where you were with him. But he seemed to look after his men well.

Or would it be better to go and see the woman where Schlumpf had had his digs?

A tedious rag this *Gerzensteiner Advertiser*. "Published twice weekly with the following supplements: Women, House and Home, Agriculture." Agriculture? For some reason the word irritated Studer. Why not "Farming"? But what was this?

Just before going to press we heard of the tragic death of Wendelin Witschi, 50, a highly respected member of the community, who was the victim of a vicious murder. Herr Witschi was known far and wide for his staunch devotion to duty and he will be remembered for many years to come. He was a citizen of the old school — Studer stroked his moustache, *of the old school*, he liked that — *we will not see his like again* . . . Yes, yes, we've heard all that before. Studer skipped a few lines.

But suddenly he stopped reading. He had sensed something. Presumably the sudden silence. The whispering had stopped. Cautiously Studer peeped over the top of the newspaper. The clink of coins was to be heard. The waitress was rummaging round in the leather purse she had under her apron.

Armin was behaving as if it had nothing to do with him. Now and then he brushed back his crimped mane with a casual sweep of his right hand. The fingers of the left were drumming on the table. Now they disappeared underneath the table. How much is she giving him? Studer wondered. There was the audible rustle of a banknote.

"The bill, please," Studer said in a loud voice. The waitress's head shot up, her face bright red. Armin gave the sole customer an angry look, which Studer returned. The young man could not withstand his gaze for long and Studer nodded imperceptibly, making a mental note, "Something fishy there."

"One lunch, that's . . ." The waitress started to read out the bill, but Studer slid a five-franc piece across the table and pocketed the change without counting it.

"The bill, Berta," the young man called. He was waving a twenty-franc note.

What did the French call those fellows who lived off women?

The name of a fish, it was on the tip of his tongue . . .

Ah yes, *maquereau.*

* * *

At the point where the track branched off right from the main road was a large sign:

Tree Nursery — Standard Roses
Gottlieb Ellenberger

with an arrow indicating the direction. Studer put off his visit until later, deciding instead to turn off to the left. The path went slightly uphill, but it brought him quickly into the woods, conifers and just a few deciduous trees. The scent of pines was good for you, particularly if you had a cold, that was what his father had always maintained. In passing he glanced at the kerbstone on which Ellenberger had landed head first the previous evening. It was an ordinary kerbstone, there was no blood on it, no point in bothering with it. Studer set off up the woodland path.

It was never a good idea to plunge straight into a case, like a pig at the trough. He could be happy with what he'd achieved today. Made enough contacts, collected some pictures . . . Just like a boy collecting cigarette cards, really, but they were lovely pictures:

There was Wendelin Witschi with 210 milligrams of alcohol in his blood, which made him, for the Italian assistant pathologist with criminological interests, an "alcoholic corpse". Then "Felicitas" with a hole in her stocking and her odd behaviour towards the barber's assistant. After that the *maquereau* and his girl friend, the waitress . . .

God, people were the same everywhere. People in Switzerland tended to keep their little indiscretions very much to themselves, but as long as they didn't impinge upon other people's lives, nothing was said. And Wendelin Witschi, whose body was preserved in the Institute for Forensic Medicine, had been a citizen of the old school. Well and good. Why not? Expressions like that were part and parcel of life and the people they were applied to just carried on and no one got worked up over their little misdemeanours, or even their not-so-little ones. Unless that is . . .

Unless something unexpected happened. Such as a murder. And a murder needed a murderer, like bread needed butter. Otherwise people would complain. And if the presumed guilty party tries to hang himself, and a detective comes along who is stubborn as a mule, then it can happen that all the little irregularities there are in everyone's life suddenly become important. You work with them, like a bricklayer with bricks, to erect a building. A building? Let's say a wall just for the moment.

Studer stopped at the edge of the woods, wiped his forehead and looked out over the countryside. A buzzard was perched on a telegraph post, taking a quiet rest. But then a crow appeared and started to pester it. The buzzard flew off, but the crow followed it, cacawing in its unpleasantly hoarse voice. The buzzard was silent. It flew higher and higher, plunging into the wind, scarcely flapping its wings at all. The crow followed. It was determined to have its squabble, it wouldn't leave off, and kept on divebombing the silent bird. But eventually it had to give up. The buzzard had reached a height where the crow no longer felt happy. With one last caw, it dropped down. The buzzard glided in a perfect circle, and Studer envied it. Down here you couldn't escape the crows with such effortless ease.

He went deeper into the woods, and the woods were very quiet . . . How far had he gone? Above his head there was a soft rustling as a light breeze played with the treetops.

Then the gentle rustle was interrupted by a different noise. Twigs cracking, a groan — as if a wounded beast were painfully dragging itself along. Rounding a thicket, Studer found a man lying on his front, whimpering. The seam at the back of his coat was split, his hair dishevelled, his shoes caked in mud.

The man had his face on his arm and was crying, the tears dampening the earth. For a moment another picture appeared in Studer's mind: Schlumpf pressing his eyes into the crook of his arm. Then he tapped the man on the shoulder and asked, "What's wrong?"

The man slowly rolled over onto his back and blinked, but said nothing. Studer recognized Cottereau, Ellenberger's head gardener.

When he asked him again what had happened, the whimpering started up once more. But now the words could be clearly heard.

"Oh my God, my God. Jesus, it's good someone's come along at last. A man could die in these woods. Oh, oh, I feel all dizzy, the thrashing they gave me . . ."

Who had beaten him up, Studer wanted to know. At that the wailing stopped and a left eye squinted up at him slyly — the other was so bruised and swollen it was hardly visible — and Cottereau said in a calm voice, "You'd like to know, wouldn't you? But you'll get nothing out of me. It was . . . perhaps it was . . . It was nothing, nothing at all. You could help me up and take me home, I'm soaked through as it is, a night out in the woods . . . It's true they . . . The boss will be waiting for me. Was he very worried about me?"

"He had a search message put out for you on the radio," Studer said. At that the man shot up, his face twisting in a grimace of pain, which was quickly replaced by an expression of pride.

"On the radio?" he asked, adding an admiring, "Ah, that Ellenberger . . . How is the boss? Was he badly hurt?"

Studer shook his head and said in a stern voice that he would leave Cottereau lying there if he refused to reveal who had attacked him.

"You do as you please, Sergeant," said the fat man, took out a pocket mirror and began to comb his hair. "Right, now you can take me home. After all, it's your fault they beat me up like this. But Cottereau's tough and he knows what he owes his boss."

Then, after a pause, he went on, "I'm getting old, I'm not the man I used to be. Pity the boss wasn't with me last night, he would have given those lads something to think about."

"Lads?" Studer asked. "What lads?"

"Heheh," Cottereau cackled, "you'd like to know, wouldn't you, Sergeant. But I'm not saying anything. I'm going to call it a day . . . Yes, enough's enough, I'm going to call it a day." Despite the pain it obviously caused him, he shook his head vigorously.

Studer bent down. Cottereau put his arm round the sergeant's shoulders, pulled himself up with much groaning and started to walk slowly, Studer supporting him.

"My back!" the fat man moaned. "Did they beat me up! And they kept saying, 'So a detective from the city's going to stick his nose in our affairs, is he?' It was just a taster, they said, to make me keep my mouth shut. 'We've got our gendarme,' they said, 'we don't need some plod from the big city.' Yes, that's what they said. And no one's going to get anything out of me, d'you hear? I'm keeping mum. As silent as the grave . . ." This was followed by more incomprehensible mutterings.

If Studer imagined he was going to get an explanation of the whole affair from Ellenberger, he was disappointed. Ellenberger was sitting on a bench outside his house. It was a kind of villa, fairly new, with a shed behind it and the shimmer of greenhouse windows. Ellenberger had a large white bandage round his head.

"Oh," he said, "so *you've* found Cottereau? Thank you, Sergeant. You're a real *deus ex machina*." He gave a grating laugh when he saw the look of surprise on Studer's face.

"Why did you get the radio to send out a search message?" Studer asked, curious.

"You'll see why later," Ellenberger said, stroking his white turban. "Maybe I did you a good turn when I did that."

"A good turn?" Studer was getting annoyed. "Cottereau's refusing to speak. And you've said nothing. Who was it attacked you? Who dragged off your head gardener?"

"Sergeant," said Ellenberger, putting on a serious look, "there are apples and apples. Some you can eat straight from the tree, they're ripe already, others have to be stored, are only ready to be eaten in February, or in March . . . Wait, Sergeant, wait until the apple's ripe. Be patient. Do you follow me?"

And Studer had to be content with that piece of advice. He didn't even have the opportunity to renew his acquaintance with Schreier and Buchegger. They were still working. A tree nursery wasn't like the civil service, Ellenberger remarked waspishly. Here they worked on Saturday afternoons . . .

Room to let

Schlumpf had told the sergeant he had digs with a couple by the name of Hofmann who ran a shop selling basketwork in Bahnhofstrasse.

The place wasn't difficult to find. On the pavement outside the shop were woven planters simply longing for a drawing-room and the obligatory aspidistra. Studer went in. The muffled jingle of a bell could be heard in the back and a woman came out into the shop. She was wearing a blue-striped smock apron, her hair was grey and neatly done. She asked how she could be of help to him; the formality sounded acquired.

He had come, Studer replied, to ask her a few questions about Erwin Schlumpf, who had lodged there. Sergeant Studer of the cantonal police. He was in charge of the case and anything she could tell him about the lad would be of help.

The woman nodded. A sad expression appeared on her face.

A terrible case, she said, and invited the sergeant in. She was alone, her husband was out doing his rounds, trying to sell their baskets. Would he mind coming into the kitchen, she'd just made some coffee, he was welcome to a cup if he liked?

A cup of coffee was exactly what Studer would like.

And he didn't regret it. It was good, not the tasteless dishwater they served in the Bear. The kitchen was small, white, very clean. Only the chair on which Studer

59

had sat down was a little too narrow. Studer began his cautious questioning.

Had Schlumpf paid his rent punctually?

Oh yes, at the end of every month, when he'd been paid, he'd come and put the twenty-five francs on the table.

"And he always stayed in in the evenings?"

"For the first year, yes, but since last year he's been coming back late quite a lot."

"Aha," said Studer. "A girl?"

Frau Hofmann smiled. A warm, motherly smile. Studer responded to the woman with a glow of pleasure. She nodded

But the girl had never come to see Schlumpf in his room?

No, never. She wouldn't allow that. Not that she had anything against it herself, but in a village . . . The sergeant would understand, she was sure . . .

The sergeant did understand. Now it was his turn to nod and he did so with conviction. He sat there in his favourite posture, legs apart, arms resting on his thighs, hands clasped. His narrow head was lowered.

"And the girl never came to call for Schlumpf?"

"No . . . that is, yes, once . . . Wednesday evening."

"What time?"

"At half past six. Erwin had just come back from work . . . He was having a wash in his room when she came into the shop. The lassie was very pale, but that didn't surprise me at all, her father had just been found murdered, hadn't he? She said she had to speak to Erwin and would I could call him. He came down and I left the pair of them alone in the kitchen, but they didn't talk for more than a minute before the girl left again. And Erwin didn't get back until after midnight."

60

"That was on Wednesday, that is the evening of the day when the body was discovered, yes?"

"Yes, Sergeant. I didn't sleep very well that night and at four in the morning I heard Erwin creeping down the stairs in his stockinged feet. And at seven Murmann arrived to arrest him. But by that time he was well away."

Erwin . . . There was a tenderness in the name as it came from the lips of the grey-haired woman. So Schlumpf had been with the same people for two years. He must have behaved himself or they presumably wouldn't have let him stay for so long . . .

"You knew about his past?"

"Ach," said Frau Hofmann. "He'd just been unfortunate. My father always used to say, 'Judge not, that ye be not judged.' No, no, I don't go to one of the Bible-bashing chapels, but you know how things can happen, sergeant. The second week he was here Erwin told us everything, his burglaries and Thorberg and the reformatory. His mother came to see him once. A decent woman . . . Erwin thought a lot of his mother. Have you seen his mother?"

Studer nodded. He heard the calm, old woman's voice asking, "But he can have his breakfast first, can't he?"

The bell above the kitchen door jangled shrilly. That would be someone in the shop, Frau Hofmann said as she stood up. But first she refilled Studer's cup and then, telling him to help himself to milk and sugar, went to serve the customer.

Studer drank the coffee in little sips until the cup was empty, then took out his watch. Almost six. Still plenty of time.

He wandered round the little kitchen, his hands clasped behind his back, his mind a blank, just shaking his head from time to time when a thought tried to pester him. He had passed the white dresser two or three times without really seeing it when, turning round rather too abruptly, he made painful contact with its corner. Only now did he subject the piece of furniture to a closer — and disapproving — examination. It was a white kitchen dresser, wider at the bottom with a narrower glass-fronted unit on top. A stack of plates, cups and glasses beside it, a few serving dishes. On the top shelf were some old newspapers, neatly stored, and next to them a messy heap of used wrapping paper. The doors were slightly ajar. Studer stared at the untidy pile of wrapping paper. Being bored, he took the paper out, grasping it firmly in both hands so that none would fall on the floor, placed the heap on the table and started to arrange it in a neat pile.

As he lifted up the fifth sheet (afterwards he could still remember the colour, it was blue paper, the kind used for wrapping sugar-loaves) he saw something black lying there.

Studer leant his fists on the table and, head on one side, looked at the black object. There was no doubt: a Browning, 6.5 calibre, a nice little gun.

But what was a Browning doing in Frau Hofmann's kitchen? How had it slipped in among the wrapping paper? Had Schlumpf . . .? Things would look black for him if the examining magistrate in Thun should get to hear of it.

Studer hesitated, unsure what to do. There might be fingerprints on the grip, although it was ridged and any prints would certainly not be clear enough to prove anything . . .

"Oh, what the hell," he said out loud, picked up the dainty little pistol — he had a brief vision of the hole it had made, the point of entry of the bullet in the back of Wendelin Witschi's head, a couple of inches from his right ear — and slipped it into his back pocket.

The kitchen door opened. Frau Hofmann was not alone. Sonja Witschi was with her.

He'd thought he'd tidy up a bit, to thank her for the coffee, Studer said, but that was as far as he'd got. He picked up the pile of wrapping paper, dumped it on the top shelf of the dresser then sat down again. He appeared to ignore the girl.

"In the village they already know you're in charge of the investigation, Sergeant, and Sonja here would like to have a word with you," said Frau Hofmann. And, turning to the girl, "Take a seat. There's still coffee in the pot."

Studer looked at the girl. The small face with the pointed nose and freckles at the temples looked pale and distraught. And her eye kept avoiding Studer's. It moved anxiously round the kitchen, flickered from the table, where the wrapping paper had been lying, to the dresser, where it was now. Her lips were pressed tightly together. What Studer most wanted to do was to get up, go over to the girl and stroke her hair to calm her, just like calming a dog down. But that wasn't on. She might know something about the gun that had been hidden? Had Schlumpf hidden it and told the girl where it was the evening before he ran away? But then why hadn't Sonja come sooner to get rid of it? Questions, lots of questions. Studer sighed.

Now Sonja did come over to him. She seemed to recognize him as the man on the train who had made the remark about Felicitas Rose. At least, she blushed when she shook hands with him. But perhaps there was another reason for that blush. The peaceful atmosphere of the kitchen had been disrupted. There was tension there, and it didn't come from Sonja Witschi's embarrassment (or was it fear?) alone. No, it seemed to Studer that Frau Hofmann's attitude had changed too.

The silence that had settled over the little kitchen was broken only by the ticking of the clock, a white porcelain clock with blue numbers. And the silence was gradually gnawing away at Studer's optimistic mood, a paralysing feeling of despondency was slowly seeping through him. Perhaps it was the awareness of the unaccustomed weight in his back pocket that was contributing to this growing feeling of despondency.

There must have been some other customers out there as well, Studer suddenly asked.

No, not customers, Frau Hofmann shook her head. It was two gentlemen . . .

"Two gentlemen? And who might that have been?"

"The mayor and Herr Schwomm, the schoolteacher."

"And what did those gentlemen want?"

Frau Hofmann remained obstinately silent. Studer looked at Sonja, whom he still thought of as Felicitas, but the girl just shrugged her shoulders. He asked her whether she had come with the two men? Yes, she replied, she'd gone to fetch them when she'd seen the sergeant go into the shop.

Studer stood up and scratched his forehead. This was becoming more and more complicated. He guessed he wouldn't get any more out of Frau Hofmann . . . but the girl perhaps?

"*Adieu*, Frau Hofmann," Studer said in a friendly voice. "And you come along with me. We're going to have a little chat."

There was no point in having a look at Schlumpf's room. It would certainly have been cleaned and swept, and Schlumpf's things would have been packed and stowed away somewhere . . .

This was confirmed for Studer as he came out of the shop. A piece of white cardboard was dangling from one of the green shutters on the upper storey. Written on it in clumsy letters was: Room to let.

The sergeant turned back to Frau Hofmann, pointed to the notice and asked whether she'd had any inquiries yet. Frau Hofmann nodded.

Who from?

Frau Hofmann hesitated, but then appeared to feel there was no harm in answering the question and said, "Schwomm — the teacher — said he would like the room for one of his relations who's coming to stay here for a month. And young Gerber came round too — he's the barber's assistant . . . Yes, that was all."

"And you invited both into the kitchen and gave them coffee?"

Frau Hofmann blushed and kneaded her hands in embarrassment. "When you're alone all day, you know . . ."

Studer nodded, tipped his hat and set off with his long stride. Sonja Witschi trotted along beside him, her high heels clattering on the asphalt. But she had changed her stockings. At least now there was no hole to be seen above the heel of her right shoe . . .

At the Witschis'

The house was a little away from the centre of the village, on a rise, surrounded by a small estate but older than the buildings around it. The door to the shop was next to the house door, on the left; beside it was a kind of open verandah with a picture of a lake in front of snowy mountains painted on the wall behind. The snowy mountains were pink, like watery raspberry ice cream. Emblazoned in fancy lettering over the door were the words, "Step right in, a welcome guest/ Brings good luck and happiness."

Below the first-floor windows was the name of the house: Mon Repos. Above the shop window, in which colourful Maggi adverts were fading, hung an equally weather-worn sign: W. Witschi-Mischler Grocer. The garden was running wild, there were tall weeds among the peas, which hadn't been tied up. A rusty rake was leant against the corner of one of the walls.

All the way there Studer had said nothing, waiting for the girl to start speaking. But Sonja had stayed silent as well. Just once she said shyly, "Even this morning in the train I thought you'd come from Bern because of Erwin, I thought you were from the police . . ." Studer had nodded, waiting for what was to follow. "And when I saw you go to see Frau Hofmann in her shop, I went to fetch Uncle Aeschbacher. Frau Hofmann's a bit of a gossip . . ."

Studer said nothing, just shrugged his shoulders. Suddenly things didn't look so promising. He wished he'd discussed the matter a bit more thoroughly with Murmann that morning.

Schwomm, the teacher, and Gerber, the barber's assistant (so the lad who read John Kling novels and had girls give him fountain pens was called Gerber), had both been in Frau Hofmann's kitchen. And Sonja. And Schlumpf, of course . . .

Who had hidden the gun? Why had it been hidden there of all places? Had someone hoped Frau Hofmann would find it and take it to the police? If Frau Hofmann had found it, then of course she would have picked it up and, curious as women are, examined it. That would have meant no useful fingerprints could have been taken from it. So it wasn't that bad, Studer reassured himself, that he'd just stuck it in his pocket without taking any precautions . . . Pity he hadn't asked Frau Hofmann when Schlumpf had come home on Tuesday evening, or, rather, Tuesday night. But no, it wasn't really necessary for him to ask her that, the answer must be in the file . . . yes, that was right, Studer remembered a page where it said, *When questioned, Frau Hofmann stated that the accused did not return home on the night of the murder until about one o'clock.* Studer shook his head. Strange. It was incriminating, and yet it didn't interest him at all. It was all too simple: a man with a record, but without an alibi, of course, the murdered man's money's found on him, he refuses to talk but insists he's innocent, then he tries to commit suicide. It sounded . . . yes, the whole thing sounded like a cheap novel.

But of course the innocent man wrongly accused was a real person, a man who'd had a hard time of it, who'd got back on the straight and narrow for a while and who now . . . What did Schlumpf read in his spare time? Another Felicitas Rose fan? Or John Kling? It would be interesting to find out. The girl would know, the girl who'd given away an expensive fountain pen . . . Was she having an affair with Gerber? It didn't look like it. But then why the expensive present?

The fountain pen . . . Yes . . . Men generally kept their fountain pen in the left-hand breast pocket of their jacket, or in their top waistcoat pocket. They usually had them on them, especially when they were travelling round taking orders. Had Wendelin Witschi had it with him on Tuesday? But then when had he given it to his daughter? Wendelin Witschi's pockets had been empty and there hadn't been any pine needles on the back of his jacket.

The kitchen. Unwashed crockery in the sink. A plate on the table with butter on it, a comb beside it.

Studer was alone. Sonja had disappeared.

The sergeant went through the open door into the next room. The curtains were grey, there was a layer of dust on the piano. The door shut behind him. It was a draughty in this house. The slamming of the door released a cloud of grey from the picture over the piano. It was a picture of the late Wendelin Witschi in his younger days, presumably taken at the wedding. A tiny black button peeped out from between the points of his stiff collar. Even then the moustache had been a pathetic affair. And his eyes . . .

On the table, on the fringed red-yellow-and-blue tablecloth, were a lot of magazines. The heavy black sideboard was covered in magazines too.

Studer flicked through them. They were all of the same type: pictures of dogs or children, a chapel in the mountains, a serialized novel, Tips for the Housewife, Analyse your Handwriting. And on the cover of every one, in letters it was impossible to ignore, *To all our policy-holders . . . Payment on death or total disability . . .*

Five different magazines. If they paid out on all the policies, that would make . . . that would make a tidy sum. And what had Münch said? Old Ellenberger had IOUs he wanted to call in?

Footsteps could be heard going to and fro upstairs. What was Sonja doing up there? Why had she left him alone down here? A heavy object was moved. Studer smiled. The poor girl must be making the beds, now, in the evening. A well-organized family, the Witschis.

Studer continued to leaf through the magazines. He came across some passages that were underlined and read:

A hot wave swept over her, burning. She threw herself into his arms, she clung to him as if she would never let go again, ever . . .

And then:

"Sonja, my dearest darling, my wife, my all — we will be happy, happy for . . ."

Deathly pale, the blood drained from her lips and trembling all over, Sonja faced him . . .

Studer sighed. He thought of lukewarm coffee for breakfast, of a woman with a soulful expression on her face because she had spent the night reading romantic novels.

Then he went over to the piano. On it, immediately below the picture of Wendelin Witschi, was a vase with wax roses and a few twigs with autumn leaves. Witschi looked as if he was squinting down at the vase. Absent-mindedly Studer picked it up. It was surprisingly heavy — and the autumn leaves were artificial too. He gave the vase a shake. It rattled. He turned it upside down . . .

Two, four, six, ten — fifteen cartridge cases fell out. 6.5 calibre.

It had gone quiet upstairs. Studer slipped one of the cartridge cases into his jacket pocket, dropped the rest in the vase, rearranged the flowers and put the vase back where it had been.

"You must excuse me, Sergeant," said Sonja. "I just wanted to tidy up a bit upstairs, in case you need to search the house. Mother doesn't get back until after the nine-o'clock train, she has to stay at the station until then. But Armin will be back soon."

Sonja rattled on and avoided Studer's eye. But the moment he looked away, he could feel the girl's eyes on his face. As soon as he looked at her again, the lids came down over her eyes. She had a rounded forehead that protruded slightly. Her hair was brushed. She looked much neater and tidier than on the train this morning.

"Oh, by the way, Schlumpf sends his regards," Studer remarked causally. He was looking out of the window. At the bottom of the vegetable garden was an old, tumbledown shed. The posts supporting the roof were squint, some tiles were missing. The door was missing too.

Sonja was silent. When Studer turned round he saw that she was crying, crying unrestrainedly. Her face was screwed up, there were deep furrows round her pointed nose, her lips were twisted and the tears were pouring down her cheeks, forming larger drops on her chin and dripping down onto her blouse.

"Lassie!" said Studer. "Lassie!" He felt uncomfortable. All he could think of was to take out his handkerchief, go over to Sonja and clumsily try to wipe up the flow of tears.

"Over here, lassie, sit yourself down . . ."

Sonja was leaning against the sergeant, she was trembling, her shoulders sagging. Studer gave a deep sigh. "Come on, lassie, over here."

Sonja sat down. Her arms were stretched out across

the table, alongside the plate with the butter, alongside the comb.

Outside, the twilight was thickening. Studer hadn't much time left, he had to be at the Murmanns' for dinner at half past seven.

He felt sorry for Sonja. He didn't want to interrogate her. Her father was dead, her sweetheart was in prison, she had to spend the day working in Bern, her brother took money from a waitress and her mother sat in the station kiosk reading romantic novels . . .

"Erwin," said Studer gently, "Erwin told me to say hello to you."

"And do you think he's guilty?"

Studer shook his head. For a moment Sonja smiled, then the tears came again.

"He won't be able to prove he's innocent," she sobbed.

"Did you give him the money?"

Remarkable how an expression could change! Sonja stared straight ahead, out of the window, in the direction of the old tumbledown shed, its doorway a black rectangle. Stared . . . and said nothing.

"Why did you give Gerber, the barber, the fountain pen?"

"Because . . . because he knows something. . ."

"Aha," said Studer.

He had sat down at the table. The chair was too small for his heavy frame and he felt uncomfortable. Had they been living in the house for long? he asked.

Her father had had it built with her mother's money, Sonja told him. She seemed pleased to have something she could talk about. Her father had worked on the railways, as a conductor, then her mother had come into some money. Her mother came from here, from Gerzenstein, her father from the area round Lake Biel. Her mother had set up the shop and her father had continued to work on the railways. During the war the shop had done well, there hadn't been many in Gerzenstein then. So her father had had himself pensioned off. Or, rather, he had simply resigned and given up his right to a pension; he'd had a weak heart and they'd caused difficulties for him on the railway. Yes, during the war things had gone well. Later on Armin had been able to attend the senior high school in Bern, he wanted to go to university. But then there was the stock market crash and her parents had lost everything and that was it. Her mother had grown sour and her father had become a travelling salesman. But he hadn't earned much. And everything was so expensive! Mother wasn't very good at economizing, she kept spending the money. On medicines and stuff like that. Uncle Aeschbacher had helped out once or twice . . . The last few words came out haltingly.

"What has Uncle Aeschbacher got to do with all this?" Studer asked.

Silence.

"You went to fetch him when you saw me go to Frau Hofmann's?"

A tormented expression. Studer felt sorry for her. He wouldn't ask her any more questions. Well, just one.

"Who is this teacher, Schwomm?"

Sonja blushed and tried to speak but her voice gave way. She cleared her throat, looked for a handkerchief, wiped her eyes with the back of her hand, then stammered, "He teaches at the secondary school, he's clerk to the council and runs one of the departments, and he conducts the mixed-voice choir, too . . ."

"Then he'll have a lot to do with the mayor? With Uncle Aeschbacher?"

72

Sonja nodded.

"Goodbye." Studer held out his hand. "And don't cry. Things'll get better."

"Goodbye, Sergeant." Sonja held out her hand. Her nails were clean.

She didn't get up and show Studer to the door. In the hall Studer stopped and looked for his handkerchief, couldn't find it, remembered he'd used it in the kitchen, turned round and went back in without knocking.

The kitchen was empty. The door to the neighbouring room was open. Sonja was standing by the piano. She had the vase with the roses and the artificial autumn leaves in her hand and seemed to be checking its weight. Her eyes were fixed on the picture of her father.

Studer's handkerchief was on the floor beside the kitchen table. He walked over quietly, picked it up and crept back to the door.

"Goodnight, lassie," he said.

Sonja spun round. She put the vase down and collected herself. "Good night, Sergeant."

Strange, her expression reminded Studer of Schlumpf's. There was astonishment in it and a despair beyond hope.

The village policeman reports

"Do sit down, Studer," said Frau Murmann. On the table was a huge plate with slices of cold sausage and ham, there was salad and at one corner of the table, beside Murmann's place, four bottles of beer.

"And take your jacket off, Studer," said Frau Murmann before making her excuses. She had to feed the baby, she explained.

Had he found anything, Murmann asked without looking up. He was concentrating on spearing a sheaf of lettuce leaves on his fork. Then he devoted himself to chewing, a rapt expression on his face.

"I found Cottereau . . ." said Studer, subjecting a juicy piece of ham to intense scrutiny.

"Well, well," said Murmann. "Now there's thing . . ." He emptied his beer glass in one gulp. Then both were silent.

The room was very simply furnished. There was an old cupboard in the corner. It was painted in the rustic style and the garlands of roses on its doors glowed softly in the light from the over-bright bulb shaded in yellow silk.

Murmann took the plates out. Then he sat down and lit his pipe. "Right, then, tell me."

But Studer said nothing. Instead he put his hand in his back pocket, took out the gun he had found at Frau Hofmann's and placed it on the table. Then he felt in his jacket pocket, held out the cartridge case he'd found at the Witschis' so that it glinted in the light and finally asked, "Do they belong together?"

Murmann examined them, completely absorbed in his task. He nodded a few times. "Same calibre," he said quietly. "But whether this cartridge was fired from that gun is not so easy to say. That kind of thing's a bit tricky. You'd need to examine the bullet hole. Where did you find the cartridge case?"

"In a vase on the piano in the Witschis' living room. There were fifteen in the vase. It looks as if someone was doing some pretty serious practice with the gun . . ."

"Aha?" said Murmann.

"Sonja's afraid. I'm convinced there are at least four people she's afraid of: the barber's assistant, the teacher, her brother and perhaps her uncle, Aesch-bacher, as well."

"Yes," said Murmann, "I can believe that. Sonja believes her father committed suicide. But if that is correct, then the insurance won't pay out. And Gerber, the barber, has noticed there's something not quite right about the supposed murder. So Sonja's afraid he might say something. D'you follow?"

"Just tell me the story from the very beginning. It's not so much facts I need as the air these people breathe, so to speak. You know what I mean? The little details no one pays any attention to, but which can illuminate the whole case . . . Illuminate! . . . As far as that's possible, of course."

So, interrupted by long pauses, with many digres-sions and interjections of "Yes?" and "D'you see?", Corporal Murmann told Sergeant Studer the following story:

Wendelin Witschi had got married twenty-two years ago. At the time he worked on the railways. Initially the couple had a flat in Aeschbacher's house, then an aunt of Frau Witschi had died, leaving her quite a lot of money. They had decided to build their own house—

"By the way," Studer asked, "what's Frau Witschi's first name?"

"Anastasia. Why d'you ask?"

Studer smiled. After a while he said, "No reason. Go on with the story."

So they'd built the house, had children, seemed to be happy. Frau Witschi wasn't afraid of work, she looked after the garden, served in the shop. Of an evening you could see the pair of them sitting contentedly on a bench outside the house, Witschi reading the paper, his wife knitting . . .

Studer could picture it clearly in his mind's eye: underneath the first-floor windows the name of the house, Mon Repos, was still shiny and new, as was the little rhyme over the door, "Step right in, a welcome guest/ Brings good luck and happiness." Wendelin Witschi was sitting on the bench, his shirt-sleeves rolled up; now he put the newspaper down (he would surely only read the *Gerzensteiner Advertiser*), stood up, went to retie a branch that had come loose on the trellis, went back . . . The two children were crawling round in the sand. Not a breath of wind. The air was heavy with the scent of new-mown hay. The woman said, "D'you know, Wendelin . . ." Peace, utter peace. The shop bell jangled. They got up, unhurried, went into the shop together, chatted with the customer about the weather, politics . . . Wendelin (Was that what his wife called him? It was something he ought to know . . . Or Father? That sounded more likely.), Wendelin Witschi had his thumbs in the armholes of his waistcoat, he was a respected citizen, related to the mayor, owned his own home. And then, year by year, the changes. His wife growing sour, spending her time reading novels, the financial problems, his son siding with his mother, the garden getting overgrown, Wendelin Witschi doing his rounds, taking to schnapps, the magazines from the insurance companies . . . The sum paid out for total disability was as much as for death . . . But the picture that stuck in Studer's mind was the bench outside the house, the children playing on the ground, the loose branch swaying in the wind and Witschi tying it up with a piece of yellow raffia . . .

For a while Studer had stopped listening, but he pricked up his ears when Murmann said, ". . . and he used to have a dog. Once, when Witschi was going home, half drunk, some lads jeered at him. The dog barked and went for them. One hit it with a stone and killed it . . ."

That fitted. Witschi feeling lonely, keeping a dog. Probably the only creature that didn't moan at him, the only creature he could pour out his heart to. Once more Studer was immersed in his daydream. He saw the Witschis sitting round the table, in the living room he'd seen. The dusty piano in the corner. Witschi trying to read the paper. And his wife's bickering. They were insured. All that money they'd paid the insurance. It never occurred to her that so far she was the only one who had got anything out of the insurance: all those magazines with the novels in them. The novels must be for Anastasia Witschi what schnapps was for her husband. An escape from their wretched situation, an escape into a world of countesses and lords who were called Horst, castles with moats and swans, fine clothes and love which declared itself in words such as, "Sonja, my own true love . . ."

Murmann had been silent for some time. He didn't want to disturb Studer's dreaming. Suddenly Studer noticed the silence. He came to with a start.

"Go on, go on, I'm listening."

"That wasn't what it looked like," Murmann said. "What were you thinking about so deeply?"

"I'll tell you later. Describe the two days. The discovery of the body, the investigation, Schlumpf's disappearance . . ."

"There's not much to tell, at least not much more than's in the files. Just a moment . . ." Murmann got up to fetch the files.

There was profound silence in the room. Studer went to the window and opened it.

There was a humming, he could hear it distinctly in the night. It was a folk song he knew. A little girl's voice had sung it yesterday, outside the window of a prison cell, "My angel art thou . . ."

The humming was trickling down through the darkness. Frau Murmann singing her baby to sleep.

Corporal Murmann came back, some loose sheets of paper in his hand. He sat down, spread them out in front of him and started. Studer stayed by the window, leaning against the wall.

Cottereau — by the way, how had Studer found Cottereau? Studer waved the question away. Later.

"Cottereau came dashing into the station, babbling on, all confused, something about a body in the woods, someone having been murdered.

"I telephoned the cantonal police commissioner before I went out and he promised to come. At my door I found the mayor, Aeschbacher, and he was accompanied by Schwomm. There was nothing odd in that, Schwomm's the clerk to the local council. The two of them insisted on coming with me, Aeschbacher wanted to take charge of the investigation. He chose the wrong person there. I don't take orders from anyone. But I got the photographer in the village to come along."

So there were five of them who set off for the scene of the crime: the mayor, Schwomm, the photographer and Murmann, with Cottereau leading the way. When they arrived, Murmann had got the photographer to take a few pictures and the man had done well.

"Definitely," Studer said, "he did a good job there. Did you notice there were no pine needles on the back of Witschi's jacket?"

Murmann shook his head. It hadn't struck him. But if Studer had noticed, then that was the main thing. The mayor kept trying to stick his oar in, telling him it was murder, robbery with murder and the culprit would be none other than one of those criminals Ellenberger had taken on. Of course with the crowd there was round the corpse the commissioner had no problem finding the place. Then they fetched Dr Neuenschwander, who officially confirmed Witschi was dead and had the body taken to the village hospital. Murmann had insisted the autopsy should be carried out at the Institute for Forensic Medicine. Dr Neuenschwander got a bit annoyed at that. He'd eventually agreed, but he drew up a report and headed it "Autopsy Report"; he'd examined the wound with a probe and described the probable place the bullet had lodged in fancy medical jargon.

"Witschi's pockets were empty?"

"Completely empty," said Murmann. "And I found that odd."

"Why?"

"I don't really know . . ."

"But Witschi was supposed to have had three hundred francs on him, wasn't he? He'd collected some debts? And he'd taken some money with him from home?"

"As to taking money with him from home, I'd be willing to swear he hadn't. But he certainly had a hundred and fifty francs with him. I telephoned the farmers he collected the debts from and they confirmed it."

"Go on," said Studer. He'd lit a Brissago.

The commissioner was a timid little thing, Murmann continued, he'd agreed to everything Aeschbacher said. The mayor kept insisting it was murder and that had struck him as odd. For his part he was sure Witschi had killed himself.

"Not very likely," said Studer. "The assistant pathologist demonstrated it to me. There'd be traces of powder. Now Witschi did have long arms, agreed, but just imagine how he'd have to have held the gun . . ." He stepped under the light, picked up the Browning on the table, checked the safety catch was on (the magazine was empty, but you never know) raised it . . . Studer tried to copy the position the Italian doctor had shown him but, his arm being rather fat, he couldn't.

Murmann shook his head. Witschi had been looselimbed, so at least there was a possibility . . .

"Get on with the story," Studer interrupted.

There wasn't much more to tell, the corporal said. On the governor's orders he had interrogated Ellenberger's employees that afternoon, but nothing of interest had come out. Then he'd gone to the Witschis', but only the son had been at home. He'd refused to comment. Eventually Armin had said he'd heard his father had been murdered in the woods, but that was the police's business, not his.

"That did make me wonder. I'd specifically sent the photographer up there that morning to prepare the family. And then, just imagine, the lad told me it was a good thing his father was dead, otherwise he'd have had to be locked up in an institution pretty soon . . ."

"And the three hundred francs?"

"After that I went to the station kiosk to question Frau Witschi. She told me her husband had taken a hundred and fifty francs with him when he left in the morning. I asked why he took so much money, but she just kept saying her husband needed it. That was all she would say, except that, just like her son, she said her husband had been getting more and more unbearable, he'd drunk more and more and Aeschbacher thought they ought to get him committed. She'd stopped giving her husband money, but Ellenberger kept stepping in, accepting IOUs. That's all well and good, I said, but then how come Witschi'd taken a hundred and fifty francs with him when he'd set off that morning? Where had he got those from? Then she realized she'd contradicted herself. She stammered something about her husband absolutely having to have them so she'd given him all the money she had left. Then she refused to say any more."

"So you think Witschi needed three hundred francs for some specific purpose?"

"Yes. Look, that would simplify the whole thing: Witschi shoots himself in the woods. He's made a rendezvous with Schlumpf there for, let's say, eleven o'clock. Schlumpf is to pick up the Browning — if it's found beside the body no one will believe it's murder. Schlumpf is to hide the gun and, if necessary, get himself accused. That's what he gets the three hundred francs for. And to soften him up, they promise he can marry Sonja once his innocence has been proved. The poor fool swallows it and now he's in the shit . . ."

"You mean his tongue is tied?"

"Of course. Otherwise he'll drag Sonja into the affair."

"Hey, Murmann . . . no, first of all tell me who it was who told you Schlumpf used a hundred-franc note in the Bear."

"I can't, I'm afraid. That evening I was writing my report in there," Murmann pointed to the neighbouring room, "when the telephone rang. I picked up the receiver and said "Gerzenstein police station,' but the person at the other end didn't give their name, just said very quickly, "Schlumpf used a hundred-franc note to pay for a drink in the Bear." When I asked who was speaking, there was just a click. The other person had hung up."

"What did you do then?"

"There was no point in hurrying. I finished my report then did the rounds of all the bars at midnight. In the Bear I took the landlord to one side and asked him if it was true that Schlumpf had paid with a hundred-franc note. The landlord said yes, that evening, at around nine o'clock. Schlumpf had ordered a half litre of red wine, then a brandy, then two large beers and on top of all that another brandy! I was surprised Schlumpf had drunk so much and I asked the landlord if Schlumpf was in the habit of hitting the bottle like that. The landlord said no, he wasn't, he'd been surprised himself. He suggested that perhaps Schlumpf would have to give up Sonja, now her father was dead . . . I telephoned to ask if I should arrest him and the commissioner said yes, but when I went to get him in the morning, the bird had flown. That's when I telephoned police headquarters."

"Yes," said Studer. "So on Friday I had the honour of arresting Schlumpf. And Schlumpf's room, you did search it? . . . Did you find anything?"

Murmann shook his bull's head. "Nothing," he said. "At least nothing incriminating."

"Were there books in the room?"

Murmann nodded.

"What kind of books?"

"Oh, you know, paperbacks with lurid covers and titles like *Love Finds a Way* and *Wrongly Accused.*"

"Are you sure one was called that?"

"*Wrongly Accused?* Yes, quite sure. Then there were some of those detective stories. *John Kling* I think they were called. You know, cheap thrillers."

"Yes," said Studer, "I know . . ."

For some time he'd been standing in the shadows again, by the window. Now he turned round. Cars were rushing past on the road outside. After Studer had watched the lights of three cars sweep past, he asked quietly, without turning round, "Aeschbacher's got a car, hasn't he?"

"Yes," said Murmann. "You mean because of the business with Cottereau? But you're wrong there. Ellenberger came to get me after the accident, after he'd been knocked down with Cottereau. The old chap looked in a bad way. Naturally I rang the mayor immediately and he came with his car. He brought Gerber along too. You know, the barber's assistant. He went on his motorbike and I was with Aeschbacher in his car. We spent all night driving round looking for Cottereau. Before we left I rang up Bern and told them to keep an eye open for stolen cars. But we didn't find anything. Where did you find Cottereau?"

"In the woods," said Studer reflectively. "Just where you weren't looking for him. But he refused to say anything."

Silence. A wireless could be heard blaring away in the house on the left. It sounded like the barking of a dog with a sore throat.

"Murmann," Studer suddenly said, "Ellenberger told you to get the radio people to make a missing-person announcement about Cottereau, didn't he?"

Murmann nodded. "I just passed the message on to police headquarters, they arranged it."

"I think I'll see if we can get the apple to ripen a bit more quickly."

Murmann stared at his colleague. The kind of things Studer came out with! But Murmann hadn't been there to hear Ellenberger say, ". . . others have to be stored, are only ready to be eaten in February, or in March . . . Wait, Sergeant, wait until the apple's ripe . . ."

But Studer hated having to wait too long. Afterwards he was to wish he'd taken Ellenberger's advice. The two requests he phoned through to Bern produced such bizarre results that they only further confused an affair that was tangled enough already. But of course Studer couldn't know that at the time.

"There'll be music in the Bear tomorrow, your friends are playing," said Murmann as Studer was about to leave. "Aeschbacher'll be there, Ellenberger too . . ."

"Sounds as if it could be fun," said Studer. Then he asked what Murmann's wife's first name was, Anni or Emmy?

Neither, said Murmann. It was Ida, but he called her Idy. Did Studer have a thing about women's Christian names?

Studer shook his head. "Just a habit," he said, grinning to himself. "Goodnight."

He took a few steps, but then turned back. "Murmann," he said, "did you search Frau Hofmann's kitchen?"

"I had a quick look. I thought I might find the gun."

"Do you remember, the dresser, on the top shelf there was a pile of wrapping paper . . ."

"Oh yes, I remember that very well. There was a sheet of that blue paper they use for wrapping up sugar loaves. I took the pile down while Frau Hofmann was away in the shop and went through it. There was nothing there. Why do you ask?"

"Because I found that," Studer pointed to his back pocket, "underneath the blue paper."

"Well I . . ." said Murmann. He took out his tobacco pouch and filled his pipe. "Well I . . ." he said again.

"The people who have been in that kitchen since you were there are: Sonja, Schwomm, Gerber — but definitely not Erwin Schlumpf. Right, I'm off to the Bear now."

"Eleven o'clock," said Murmann puffing out clouds of tobacco smoke, "you watch out. Aeschbacher's sure to be there, playing Jass . . ."

The thumbprint

It was a cool night. Studer shivered on the short walk from the police house to the Bear. His cold was back. His head was stuffed up and he had an unpleasant tickle in his throat, so he decided to have a final drink, a hot toddy. But he didn't want to sit in the main bar. He asked the landlord, who was standing in the doorway, whether there was a side room where he could sit. The landlord nodded.

The door to the main bar was left open. It was pretty noisy through there, a buzz of voices overlaid with scraps of melody from the wireless ("Good, it's switched on," thought Studer). Then a voice said, "Fifty for a run of four to the ace of trumps, plus the marriage, twenty for the seven, eight, nine of trumps . . ." Cries of admiration were interrupted by the same voice saying, ". . . and the tricks're all mine."

The tone of voice reminded him of something, but he only realized what it was when he heard the radio announcer say, "And now, for the final number in our concert of light music . . ." Of course the announcer was speaking formal German, not dialect, but his tone of voice, his way of speaking was the same as that of the voice that had declared the outrageous hand.

The landlady brought his hot toddy and sat down at the table, asking how things were going, whether he was making any progress with the investigation. Of course Schlumpf was the murderer, she thought, but there were others to blame for the fact that crimes like that could happen in a quiet little village like Gerzenstein . . .

It was eerie. As he listened to her talking, Studer had the impression he was hearing Gritli Wenger yodelling on the radio. Then the landlord came and joined them — he looked much younger than his wife, he had bandy legs and, as it later turned out, was a sergeant in the dragoons — and when he began speaking his voice really and truly was the voice of the comic, Hegetschweiler, from the *Cabaret Cornichon*.

What had the people done with their own voices? Had they been infected by the radio? Had the wireless sets in Gerzenstein triggered off a new epidemic: voice-swapping?

There it was again!

In the other room someone was complaining he hadn't got anything to drink. But he spoke those simple words in such a lilting accent, Studer thought he was listening to the popular song, "I haven't got a motor car, I haven't got a big estate . . ."

Cautiously Studer got up and went over to the door, staying partly hidden behind the door-post, where he had a view of the whole room.

Four men were sitting at the table where he had had his lunch. The most striking was the one who had squeezed himself into the corner. A fat man, heavily built. A bristly tom-cat moustache jutted out over his top lip, his face was red, his forehead came to a point at the top, his chin was embedded in folds of fat. His whole head was on fire, one lone lock of brown hair fell down over his forehead.

Who was that man, there, Studer asked the landlady.

The one with the pointed head? That was Aeschbacher, the mayor. Studer smiled. He recalled

Ellenberger's brief but telling characterization: like a pig with scarlet fever. But it wasn't quite right, Studer thought to himself. Aeschbacher had remarkable eyes, very, very remarkable eyes. Crafty, clever . . . No, definitely *not a* day-old calf.

The mayor's partner was a man who seemed to have a huge, bright yellow sponge where his head ought to have been. Studer could only see him from behind, but he could hear his voice:

"I'm going to have to pass, I'm afraid."

It was the voice that had complained just now that he had nothing to drink, the voice that sounded like a comic song.

"And who's that playing with the mayor?"

"That's Schwomm, the teacher."

A fitting name, thought Studer. Just change one letter and it'd be *Schwamm* and from behind his head, with its mass of blond curls, did look like a sponge. He was wearing a high, stiff collar, his dark jacket was definitely made to measure. From where he was standing Studer could also see his hands. The tiny hairs on them shimmered in the lamplight.

At another table were four young men. Armin Witschi was one and the barber's assistant another. The other two were still youngsters, really, with down on their cheeks and trousers that were too short; the way they were sitting they rode up over their calves. They were playing cards too. The wireless had just announced, "That was the end of our evening concert." No one looked up. The voice continued, "Before the weather forecast, we have an announcement from the cantonal police concerning Jean Cottereau, head gardener at the Ellenberger tree nursery who was reported missing this morning." Studer knew what the announcer was about to say. The people in Bern had lost no time getting his message broadcast. Now he was curious to see what effect it would have.

"Herr Cottereau has been found. He was unable to give any information as to who had attacked him nor why he had been abducted, but Sergeant Studer, who is in charge of the investigation into the murder of Wendelin Witschi in Gerzenstein, is convinced there is a connection between the murder and the attack on Cottereau and Ellenberger. Anyone with information relevant to this case is asked to report to the gendarmerie post in Gerzenstein or to telephone police headquarters in Bern."

Silence.

Studer had stepped out into the doorway to observe the effect of the announcement.

The four lads seemed transfixed. The last trick was lying on the black baize cloth, almost exactly in the middle, four cards on top of each other, but no arm stretched out to pick them up. They kept their cards clutched to their chests.

At the mayor's table no one seemed affected. The cards had just been dealt. Aeschbacher held his in one hand, the other supporting his massive red head. His lips were slightly twisted, his moustache stuck out at all angles.

The radio announcer continued, "It is expected the public prosecutor's office will ma—"

Aeschbacher waved his hand and said, in the voice that was so similar to the announcer's, "I've heard enough of that prattle. Off."

The waitress seemed to have been waiting just for that command. A click. Silence.

The wooden tables, freshly scrubbed, shone brightly, with the black squares of the baize cloth for cards in the middle. The yellow gleam of the two ceiling lamps, swathed in clouds of blue smoke, was reflected in the carafes. Distinctly Studer heard the sound of a match being struck on the ribbed strip of the pottery ash-tray. Aeschbacher relit his cigar, then his voice rang out in the silence, "Give the lads there a bottle of red and put it on my bill."

Mumbling at Armin Witschi's table. "*Merci*, mayor, thanks . . ."

Then movement returned to the group. That too was a little eerie. It looked as if a set of robots had been switched on. They suddenly started to move normally again, fanned-out hands were raised in front of their eyes, cards slapped down on the table.

Aeschbacher was sitting up straight. He still had his cards in his hand, but his eyes were fixed on the young men, as if he were trying to compel them to look in his direction. But they were engrossed in their game. The waitress went over to them, pressing lovingly against Armin Witschi as she slowly placed the bottle of wine on the table. It seemed to irritate Witschi, he turned round abruptly — and noticed Aeschbacher staring at him. The mayor waved him over with the hand holding his cards. Obediently Armin stood up and went over to the older men's table. The mayor whispered urgently to him. Then Studer suddenly realized that Aeschbacher's eyes were fixed on him. The sergeant was standing alone in the doorway, the landlady had gone away, and he clearly saw the gesture with which the mayor pointed him out to Armin Witschi. Now Witschi was squinting over at the sergeant too. Studer felt uncomfortable, most of all he would have liked to go back and drink his hot toddy, it must be getting cold by now. But he wanted to watch the end of the dumb-show.

But nothing else happened.

"Trumps, Aeschbacher," said the man who looked as if he had a sponge instead of a head, the man who spoke as if he were singing a comic song, Schwomm, the teacher.

"All right, all right" said the mayor irritably. Aeschbacher gestured at Witschi to go. With a single move-ment he fanned out the cards in his hand. "Pass," he snapped. Then, addressing the waitress, "Close the door, Berti, there's a draught."

Studer went back to his hot toddy. The door to the adjoining room was closed.

*   *   *

Back in his little room, Studer undressed. Then, in his pyjamas, he stood at the window and looked out over the silent countryside. The moon was very white, from time to time clouds passed over it; the field of rye was a strange bluish colour.

The sergeant remembered an acquaintance with whom he'd worked in Paris and got on well with. Madelin was his name, he was a *commissaire* with the *police judiciaire*. A skinny, easy-going man who could put away an incredible amount of white wine without getting drunk. He had once summed up the essence of his twenty years' experience with the police to Studer as follows:

"Believe me, Studer (he pronounced it "Studaire"), I'd rather have ten murder cases in the town than one in the country. Out in the country, in a village, the people stick together, everyone's got something to hide. Nobody will tell you anything, not a thing. While in the town . . . my God, it's more dangerous, yes, but you know the customers you're dealing with straight away. They can't keep their mouths shut, they let things out. God save us from country murders."

Studer sighed. Commissaire Madelin was right.

And deep down inside he was still reproaching himself for not having handled the gun with sufficient care. Perhaps they would have been able to find some fingerprints after all? But what use would that have been? He couldn't just turn up at Schwomm's house, not to mention Mayor Aeschbacher's, with an ink-pad and the appropriate papers and ask them if they would be so good as to record their fingerprints for posterity on these official forms. Of course there were other ways of getting fingerprints, cigarette cases, for example . . . but Studer didn't smoke cigarettes and these methods were all so complicated. They were all right for books, the secret services seemed to have had some success with them, but in the real world . . . ? Studer sneezed and went to bed.

He was sitting in a huge lecture theatre, wedged into a narrow desk. The lid was sticking painfully into his belly, he couldn't stretch his legs out. It was stuffy, he couldn't breathe properly. A man in a white coat was walking restlessly up and down in front of a blackboard. He was speaking. And a huge thumbprint had been drawn in chalk on the blackboard. The lines made crazy patterns, loops, spirals, mountains, valleys, waves. Straight lines had been drawn out from the various features and been numbered. And the man dashing up and down in front of the blackboard pointed to the numbers and continued his lecture, "The capillaries stay the same, from the cradle to the grave, remember that, gentlemen, and if there's agreement on twelve points, then you have conclusive proof. This is the thumb of a man, gentlemen, a thumbprint that was lost through the carelessness of a police officer and which, with my new method of distant wave-vision, I have restored to its original form.

The culprit is there among you, I won't name him, he has been punished enough already. He will have to resign and starve in his old age, for he has been guilty of a serious dereliction of duty. This thumbprint, ladies and gentlemen . . ." Sonja Witschi was sitting in the front row. She was wearing a white dress and looking contemptuously at Studer. It pained Studer very much. But what hurt him most was the fact that Aeschbacher was sitting next to Sonja and had his arm round her shoulders. Studer wanted to hide under the bench, he could feel the eyes of the whole audience on him, but he couldn't, the desk was too narrow. Suddenly the captain of police appeared in the doorway and said in a loud voice, "Egg on your face again, Studer? Come here, come here at once." Studer pushed his way out of the row, Sonja and Aeschbacher were laughing at him, the man in the white coat had suddenly turned into the schoolteacher, Schwomm, who started singing, "That's love, that's love, a silly thing called love . . ." Aeschbacher had stuck his thumb up and it grew and grew until it was as big as the drawing on the blackboard. "Poroscopy," Schwomm shouted in his doctor's coat, "dactyloscopy!" he screamed. And Commissaire Madelin was standing by the window, an angry look on his face and cursing. "Have you forgotten Locard, Studaire? Fifteen and six and six and eleven points was enough for a conviction in the Desvignes case. And in the Witschi case? Forgotten everything, Studaire? You ought to be ashamed of yourself." But the police captain took a pair of handcuffs out of his pocket and handcuffed Studer. As he did so he said, "But I'm not going to buy you a glass of red wine in the station cafeteria. Not me!" Studer was in tears, he was crying like a little child, his nose stung as he shambled along behind the police lieutenant.

The Convict Band

With the white bandage on his head Ellenberger resembled some Indian fakir from the music hall who, having pawned the dinner jacket he wore for his act, had to go round in a borrowed suit. Though Ellenberger wasn't actually going anywhere. He was sitting in solitary silence at one of the many little round iron tables which, with their red tablecloths, looked like giant toadstools as imagined by an Expressionist painter.

The weather was sunny and warm, it even looked as though it might last. The chestnut trees in the garden of the Bear had stiff red pyramids on their branches and the petals drifted down onto the tables like red snow.

It was a large garden. At the rear, closed off by a fence, a raised floor had been put up on which two couples were dancing. The band were so close to the fence they might have been glued to it. Accordion, clarinet, double bass. As the sergeant walked across the garden to say hello to Ellenberger, he nodded to the band. The three of them returned his nod, apparently pleased. The accordion player briefly took his hand off the bass keys and waved. That was Schreier.

Schreier, whom Studer had arrested at his lodgings three years ago. The bass player waved his bow — another old friend, a cat burglar, though it was two years since the police last had the pleasure of his company.

Studer sat down at Ellenberger's table.

Hello . . . How's things . . . Lovely weather . . .

Then Ellenberger asked, with a grin on his toothless face, "Are your apples ripe yet, sergeant?"

"No," Studer said.

The beer was cool. Studer took a long pull at his glass. The band was playing a tango.

"We could be beside the lake at Zurich," said Ellenberger with the air of a connoisseur of music. He clicked his tongue as he spoke. His legs were stretched out: black silk socks and brown shoes.

"*À la vôtre, commissaire* . . ." he said, then asked the sergeant if he spoke French.

Studer nodded. He looked at Ellenberger. In some odd way, his face seemed to have changed. The features were the same, but their expression was different. As if an actor who had been playing an old peasant to perfection had suddenly abandoned the role. But from behind the mask it was not the face of an actor that appeared; what Studer saw was a thoughtful old gentleman who spoke French fluently, without an accent, accompanying his speech with delicate gestures. The skin on the back of his hands was covered in blotches the colour of withered beech leaves.

He shouldn't be surprised at his predilection for ex-convicts, he told Studer, still speaking French. He had made his money in the colonies, where he had always had prisoners allocated to him as labourers. He'd got on well with the French Resident . . . But we humans are stupid, aren't we? When he felt old age approaching he'd been filled with homesickness for Switzerland and had bought a property in this village of Gerzenstein. Actually, he said, the tree nursery he'd opened was a luxury. He didn't need the income, his money was securely invested, as securely, that was, as was possible in those insecure times.

Studer was not paying close attention to what the old man was saying. He was comparing the picture of Ellenberger he had in his mind with the old man in front of him. Even when he had first met him, last Friday evening in the cafe, sitting at the little round table by the window, with a sickly grey evening outside, he had felt strangely unsure about the man. It had seemed to Studer that everything about him was false. Everything? Not quite. The feeling Ellenberger appeared to have for Schlumpf was genuine, definitely . . .

But what was Ellenberger after today? Why was he behaving so differently? Studer gave an imperceptible shake of the head. It seemed to him that the face Ellenberger was wearing today still wasn't the genuine one. Or did the man not have a true face. Was he a kind of confidence trickster manqué? You never knew where you were with him.

Two young men and a girl sat down at a nearby table. Sonja Witschi gave him a slight nod. The two lads whispered to each other, grinned, squinted across at Studer and exchanged remarks. When the waitress brought their beer, Armin Witschi put his arm round her hips in a demonstrative gesture. She stayed at the table for a while, slowly going red, a touchingly happy expression on her tired features . . . But she was called away. She gently freed herself from the embrace. Armin Witschi patted his hair, which was piled up over his forehead in permanent waves. His little finger stuck out.

"*Un maquereau*," Studer said quietly to himself. It didn't sound disapproving, more like a friendly statement of fact.

"God, yes," Ellenberger replied with a toothless grin, "they're not as rare as you might think."

Armin Witschi gave the pair of them an angry look: He couldn't have understood the words, but he had sensed they were talking about him.

The other lad at the table was Gerber, the barber's assistant. He was wearing wide-bottomed grey flannel trousers and a blue knitted shirt with no tie. His arms were very skinny.

He stood up and bowed to Sonja. The two of them climbed onto the dance floor. Schreier, the accordionist, played a wrong note when he saw the pair of them dancing. Studer looked up and saw that the three musicians had their eyes fixed on him. He nodded to them, though he had no idea why he gave them such an encouraging nod.

The three musicians were all wearing outfits of the same colour: mustard-yellow linen trousers, mustard-yellow sleeveless pullovers and shirts that were as yellow as mustard.

Ellenberger seemed to be able to read Studer's thoughts. "Yes," he said, "I bought the outfits for them. Designed them too. I felt like giving the respectable citizens of Gerzenstein a mild shock. God, when you've got nothing to amuse you . . ."

Studer nodded. He felt less and less like talking. He pushed his chair back and sat there in his favourite posture, legs apart, forearms on his thighs, hands clasped. The garden lay in front of him, here and there sunbeams pierced the thick foliage, daubing the grey gravel with splotches of white. When the music stopped, the chirruping of the birds, invisible in the tree-tops, quivered over the buzz of voices . . .

Sergeant Studer was not happy. Things had gone too well at the beginning. Strangely enough, what bothered him most was the dream he had had the previous night. In the morning he had examined the gun.

It was a cheap model, he vaguely remembered having seen one in a window display in Bern somewhere . . . Twelve or fifteen francs? He'd telephoned head-quarters from the gendarmerie office and given the number, asking them to check with gunsmiths. Hope-less to imagine they could identify the purchaser, but they might be able to show that Schlumpf couldn't possibly have bought the Browning.

Someone had stopped in front of him. At first all he saw was two black trouser legs, very baggy at the knees. His eye moved slowly upwards: a huge stomach strain-ing over a canvas belt, a soft collar and the black knot of a tie; finally, embedded in rolls of fat, the face of the mayor, Aeschbacher.

Studer remembered his dream.

But Aeschbacher was friendliness itself. He wished them a polite good afternoon, asked whether he might join them, gave Studer a hearty handshake and took a seat, panting and puffing. Without having to be asked the waitress brought a large beer, which disappeared inside Aeschbacher, leaving a few flecks of foam on the bottom of the glass.

"Another," the mayor panted.

He patted Ellenberger's arm. The old man made a noise like a cat that doesn't quite know whether to purr contentedly or hurl itself spitting at its molester.

Aeschbacher saved the situation by asking whether they fancied a game of Jass, Zuger Jass of course?

The waitress, who had just brought the mayor's second beer, rushed off, brought the black baize cloth, spread it out on the table, placed the sharp-ened piece of chalk and the carefully cleaned slate beside it and left. Taking three empty beer glasses with her.

"Three rappen a point?" Aeschbacher suggested.

Ellenberger shook his head. The mask of the well-travelled gentleman who spoke French without an accent had been replaced by the other. It was the old peasant sitting at the table again, and it was the old peasant who said in his unpleasant croak, "Three rappen's too little. I'm not playing for less than ten."

Studer was beginning to feel uneasy. Zuger Jass was a damn dangerous game. If you had bad luck you could easily end up losing fifteen francs, and fifteen francs was not to be sneezed at. He couldn't really put losses at cards on his expenses. But he found the idea of observing the way the two behaved while playing cards so appealing that he finally nodded. Aeschbacher pulled over the slate and wrote the three initials across the top: S. E. A. Then he shuffled the cards and dealt. Ellenberger took a pair of steel-rimmed spectacles out of his jacket pocket and placed them on his nose. In the very first game Studer made a score of a hundred and fifty. He gave a sigh of relief.

"Sergeant," said the mayor, scratching at his tom-cat moustache with a fingernail, "I've heard you'll be retiring soon?"

"Yes."

"Well now," with a single movement Aeschbacher fanned out his cards and held them up in front of his face, "I might have . . . I might have an interesting job for you."

Silence. Studer took his time arranging his cards into suits. He hadn't got a single trump, but at least he had a meld of seven diamonds to the ace, which made another two hundred.

"Oh yes?" said Studer, then rapped the table with his knuckle as a sign that he was coming in. Aeschbacher was in too, but Ellenberger gently laid his hand down on the table and shook his head.

"Share?" asked Aeschbacher.

"No, I have to play, or at least keep my points in hand for myself."

"Play," said Aeschbacher and led the Jack of trumps. "A friend of mine," he went on in a confidential tone, "has opened a private detective agency and is looking for someone who's efficient, speaks several languages, has a modicum of common sense and is capable of carrying out investigations on his own. Starting as soon as possible. The police will release you immediately, just you leave that to me. I have my contacts. How about it? I can telephone tomorrow . . ."

"Oh yes?" said Studer, throwing in his cards. He could see he wasn't going to win a single trick, but the points in hand were enough anyway.

"Don't let yourself be taken in by the snake-charmer," Ellenberger said. "Snake-charmers always promise the moon but when you look at it closely, it's just a piece of mouldy cheese."

Aeschbacher gave him an angry look and told him to be so good as to keep his big trap shut. It was causing a draught.

Then the mayor should keep his proposals for a *tête-à-tête* with Studer, Ellenberger replied. If he made them in public, then he, Ellenberger, had a perfect right to express an opinion.

Studer shuffled the cards.

At the next table Armin Witschi had stood up, put his arm round the waitress's waist and taken her, resisting slightly, onto the dance floor. The barber's assistant with the red lips had got up too and taken Sonja by the arm. Sonja didn't seem very keen . . .

Studer stared at the two couples dancing cheek to cheek on the raised floor — though Sonja had placed her hand against Gerber's shoulder to try and keep a little distance between them. The band was playing and Schreier was singing, "*Grüezi, grüezi,* welcome to Switzerland . . ."

"*Allez, allez,*" said Aeschbacher impatiently, "deal." But he too turned round and watched the couples dancing.

"Ah yes, Sonja." He nodded. "A good girl."

Aeschbacher ought to know that better than anyone else, said Ellenberger softly, then burst out into that booming laughter that didn't seem to go with his scrawny frame.

The landlady appeared in the inn doorway, scanned the garden, saw the table where the three men were sitting and came over.

"You're wanted on the telephone," she said to the mayor in the voice that still sounded like Gritli Wenger yodelling.

"Am I?" said Aeschbacher, adding that perhaps he would hear something about his stolen car.

Studer pricked up his ears. When did the car disappear? he enquired

Yesterday evening, was the reply. The mayor had left it here, outside the Bear, but when he went to go home, it had disappeared. He'd forgotten to lock it.

Studer repressed an oath. He couldn't even rely on Murmann. Why hadn't he told him?

He'd be right back, Aeschbacher said as he went off with the landlady. He bore his fat belly in front of him, like a street vendor carrying a tray with his wares.

Immediately Ellenberger was the genteel friend of the French Resident once more. In his elegant French he gave Studer to understand that he should beware of the mayor.

But, Studer objected, hadn't Ellenberger said Aeschbacher was stupider than a day-old calf?

Just a figure of speech, said Ellenberger, letting the cards cascade on to the table. Aeschbacher wasn't stupid, oh no. He wouldn't be surprised, Ellenberger went on, if the theft of his car wasn't just another trick.

At that point the mayor returned. His tom-cat moustache was twisted in an unpleasant, mocking smile. "They caught the man in Thun," he said. "I have to go and collect it. And you're to go to the telephone too, sergeant. The examining magistrate wants a word with you . . ."

"What, today? On a Sunday?"

"Yes. And then you can go back to Bern this evening. The case is solved."

"Eh?" said Ellenberger.

But Aeschbacher just stuck his broad-brimmed hat on his head, said, "Goodbye," and left the garden.

* * *

It was indeed the examining magistrate on the telephone.

His first words were, "Schlumpf's confessed, Sergeant."

"Confessed?" Studer roared into the receiver. He was ready to explode. It was just one thing after another: the dream last night, the gun, the cartridge cases in the vase on the piano, the mayor's offer, the tension between Ellenberger and Aeschbacher, Sonja Witschi, Sonja especially, who was dancing with Gerber — and then, and above all, Corporal Murmann's answer to the question of whether he thought Schlumpf was guilty: *Chabis.*

And now the examining magistrate was warbling on the telephone, "Schlumpf has confessed, sergeant."

"When?" Studer asked angrily.

"After lunch today. At half past twelve if the precise time is of any interest."

Irony too! It was too much for Sergeant Studer.

"Good," he said softly, "I'll come to Thun tomorrow morning, sir."

"Do you consider that opportune?" the voice enquired.

Opportune! That word just about put the lid on it. Couldn't the man speak plain German? Why didn't he just ask if Studer thought his presence was needed? No, it had to be "opportune".

"Yes," Studer spluttered, "I even consider it necessary!"

The sound of a throat being cleared came down the line.

"It was just a thought," said the examining magistrate in conciliatory tones. "I've been speaking to the state prosecutor, you see, and he was of the opinion that any further investigation was unnecessary. We were going to get you taken off the case."

"Do go ahead," said Studer, abandoning his Swiss dialect for formal German. "However, I would advise you to have a look at the literature on confessions. There are different kinds of confession, you know . . . And you're welcome to get me taken off the case, if that's what you want. I've been thinking of taking some leave and I like this Gerzenstein very much indeed. The air is so healthy. Perhaps I'll get my wife to come and join me here. When did you catch the car thief?"

"Errm," said the magistrate. "The car thief? A policeman stopped him this morning. The man had a record . . ."

"Has he spoken to Schlumpf?"

"Er, yes, I do believe he has. We put him in the same cell."

"You don't say! Goodbye, then, sir. I'll see you tomorrow. I may be bringing an important witness with me." And with that Studer hung up.

*   *   *

There was no one dancing any more. All the tables were occupied. The waitress was dashing to and fro with sausages: slim Emmentalers, bulging caraway sausages, glistening with fat, or cervelats gleaming dully on the plate. The pots of bright yellow mustard were in great demand. Wine appeared on the tables, bottles, not glasses or carafes. Armin Witschi had ordered a bottle of Neuchâtel. Sonja was taking no more than tiny sips of hers. She looked cowed, apprehensive.

The three men from the Convict Band in their lurid yellow outfits (the arms left free by the short sleeves were sinewy and brown, their faces were brown and weather-beaten too) were sitting at a table that had been moved quite close to Ellenberger's. But Ellenberger remained sitting in solitary splendour; on the table in front of them the musicians had two bottles of wine and a large platter of ham.

Studer made his way back between jaws champing on sizzling sausages or cold ham. He caught the mocking smile on Armin Witschi's lips. Sonja was staring into space, her cheek slumped against the back of her hand; her glass was still full, the caraway sausage sweating juice untouched on her plate.

The sergeant went back to his seat at Ellenberger's table. In unison the Convict Band toasted Studer. An empty glass suddenly appeared before him. Schreier stood up, came over with the bottle and filled it. "In five minutes, outside the post office, Sergeant," he whispered, "I've got something to show you."

Studer glanced at Ellenberger out of the corner of his eye, but he seemed to have heard nothing, so he gave Schreier an unobtrusive nod (What could this be now? What did the lad know?) and clinked glasses with the three of them, Buchegger, a scrawny individual with irregular features and broad, rounded teeth, Bertel, whose second name he had forgotten but whom he vaguely remembered. Had he collared him as well at some time or other? Now he was playing the double bass and had mended his ways, to all appearances . . .

Out loud Studer said, "To the band," and emptied his glass. A stupid saying occurred to him: "Wine after beer, nothing to fear; beer after wine, just say *nein*." He couldn't get the words out of his head, so he said them out loud. The three men laughed dutifully, but as their laughter died away Studer announced quietly, "Schlumpf's confessed."

It was interesting to observe the reactions of the four. Ellenberger cleared his throat and said, just as quietly, "*Vous n'y comprendrez jamais rien, commissaire.*"

Bertel gave a start (he looked like a crafty monkey) and bellowed an oath which appealed to the omnipotence of the Saviour.

Buchegger, the skinny bear, said just one word: "Idiot!"

Schreier ran his hand through his long, dark hair, turned his head a little so that the three at the other table, six feet away, could hear him clearly, said, "Aha! so Schlumpfli's confessed, has he?" and, with a slight nod of the head invited the sergeant to observe Sonja, her brother and Gerber.

And indeed, the reaction at that table was even more interesting.

Sonja started, clenched her fist, sat up straight and stared at her brother with a look of intense hatred.

106

Armin shrugged his shoulders. Gerber went pale, his complexion, pasty enough as it was, took on a greenish tinge. He patted Sonja's arm soothingly, as if to comfort her with the thought that even if Schlumpf had had it, *he* was still there. Then an anxious look came over Sonja's face. She tried to stand up, but Armin and Gerber pulled her back down onto her seat and pressed her glass into her hand. Sonja sipped at it. She took her handkerchief out of her bag, wiped her eyes and looked in Studer's direction. Their eyes met. Studer raised his hand in a gesture of reassurance, at which a trusting smile suddenly broke across Sonja's face. Studer knew that when the time came he would be able to rely on her help.

"I'll probably have to give Schlumpf up," said Studer out loud, got to his feet, said a general farewell and strode out of the garden.

Five minutes later Schreier caught up with him. He'd taken off his musician's outfit and was wearing an ordinary suit.

Wendelin Witschi's shooting range

"I know Schlumpf well," said Schreier, matching his step to Studer's. "From the very beginning, when he first came to Ellenberger's, I told him. 'Just you be careful,' I said, 'and don't get involved with women, it always leads to trouble. A waitress, OK, but not a girl from the village.' You agree, don't you, sergeant?"

Studer muttered something and sighed. Prisoners didn't have an easy time of it when they found work outside after they'd been released. It only needed one person to recognize them, to shout "jailbird" at them. And what could they do? Make a complaint? People didn't even have to use the word itself, the direct insult, they could show the contempt they felt simply through their behaviour towards them. Most of them weren't really bad. What had Schreier been doing when Studer had arrested him? Helping his landlady shell beans . . . Ah well . . .

"What do you want to show me?" Studer asked.

"You'll see, Sergeant. Witschi committed suicide."

There it was again! Murmann thought that too . . . Suicide? . . . But, for Christ's sake, Witschi couldn't work miracles.

He did have long arms, that was true. But even assuming he'd managed to get the gun behind his right ear and hold his aim while he got his shot off, there was still one unexplained fact: the lack of powder marks. A reduced charge? Not very likely. How then? And assuming Witschi had the courage to go through with it, someone must have come along after he killed himself to pick up the gun. The Browning that had been hidden among the wrapping paper in Frau Hofmann's kitchen. By whom? Who had picked up the gun? Had it all been arranged in advance?

"What makes you think Witschi killed himself?"

"You'll see in a moment."

Cars screamed along the road, motorbikes thundered past with a splenetic roar. There was already a Sunday feel about the place. The houses looked abandoned, but they weren't silent, not even today. A squawk here, a humming there, now and then a scrap of song . . .

Gerzenstein's wirelesses were playing with the atmospheric disturbance. There was no one in to keep an eye on them, so they were getting up to all kinds of mischief, all by themselves, just to brighten up a lonely afternoon. During the week there was so much work for them. They sang, they played music, they spoke. Professors, priests, psychologists, parliamentarians — the radios dutifully parroted the words some important personage was reading from his manuscript. And the words penetrated the Gerzensteiners' skulls, softened their brains. Like steady rain on boggy ground. It was the wirelesses that controlled Gerzenstein. Didn't the mayor speak with the voice of an announcer?

At last, there was the Witschis' house. Here too there was squawking coming out through the closed shutters, so loud that at first Studer thought there was a party going on in one of the rooms. But it was only one of the lonely radios whiling away the time.

Mon Repos, in blue paint that was starting to flake off. "Step right in, a welcome guest/ Brings good luck and happiness." Why did the little rhyme sound like mockery to Studer? Happiness? Had the Witschis ever been truly happy? In his mind's eye he saw Wendelin Witschi in his shirt-sleeves, reading the newspaper, standing up, going to tie a loose shoot on the trellis . . . The shop bell ringing . . . a discussion about politics . . . And now Witschi was lying in a cold white room with a bullet hole behind his right ear.

Studer shook himself. Schreier was saying, "Along here, sergeant," as he led him through the garden towards the old, tumbledown shed, the shed with the squint posts supporting the roof. The door was missing. In its place yawned a black hole.

But inside the shed it wasn't actually that dark. Some tiles were missing. The sparse light dribbling in through the gaps blended with the darkness into a grey murk.

Broken spades, a bent rake, empty boxes, wood shavings, Persil packets, wrapping paper. Tiny, glittering motes danced in the shafts of light stretching from roof to floor.

"Well?" Studer asked. He coughed. The dust was getting into his lungs.

Schreier went over to a pile of tea-chests, carefully moved them aside and pulled out a door, presumably the door to the shed. The rusty hinges were still attached to it.

"Have you got a torch?" Schreier asked.

"Yes."

"Switch it on."

Studer shone the beam on the door. He let out a low whistle between his teeth.

Two, four, six, ten — fifteen bullet holes. Spread over the middle of the door. They were all within a rectangle of about twenty-four by sixteen inches. And the rectangle was a light patch on a door which was otherwise black with age. Studer bent down to have a

110

closer look. Yes, the rectangle had been planed, you could still see the marks . . .

But the most remarkable thing about the bullet holes was this: the first ones, in the top left-hand corner of the rectangle, showed clear scorch marks round the edges.

"Deflagration marks," said Studer softly. Five of the holes had these marks. Round the sixth they were less distinct, and they grew fainter the farther down the bullet holes were. The last three had clean edges, the wood around them was white . . .

It was a solid door. All the bullets were still in the wood. Studer took out the thin pencil he had in his notebook and began to measure the depth of the holes. He measured them several times, taking great care. He pressed his thumbnail firmly against the pencil to determine any difference in depth as precisely as possible, right down to the last fraction of an inch. All fifteen holes were of the same depth. Therefore the last bullets, the ones whose holes had clean edges, had been fired from the same distance. Why did only the first ones have scorched edges?

"Why do only the first holes have powder marks?" Studer asked out loud.

Schreier giggled. It was an unpleasant sound. It reminded Studer of prison, a jailhouse giggle. It sounded so half repressed.

"Come on, out with it, man, if you know something," he barked.

"I'm not really sure, Sergeant," said Schreier, "but you know as well as I do that if you hold a sheet of paper over the muzzle and fire, all the powder traces stick to the paper and . . ."

Studer was getting angry. "And you imagine Witschi held a sheet of newspaper over the muzzle of his gun with his left hand and then fired the shot? Would you like to demonstrate?"

Schreier shook his head. He took something out of his pocket and held it in the light. It was a rectangle of red cardboard. *Riz La Croix* was written on it. The cover of a book of cigarette papers.

"I found this here in the shed," he said diffidently. "When I was rummaging round in here. The day after Schlumpf was arrested."

"So?" Studer asked.

"None of the Witschi family roll their own. Old Witschi smoked cigars, more recently a pipe. Armin smokes English cigarettes, the ones they sell in the shop. Therefore . . ."

"Therefore . . .?" Studer asked. He was beginning to find this Schreier fellow interesting.

"I thought this might be what happened: old Witschi took a few cigarette papers, crumpled them up and stuck them in the end of the barrel. He had to test how many you needed before you got a clean bullet hole. That's why he used so many shots. Until it worked . . ."

"Makes sense," said Studer. "Complicated but not impossible."

Reflectively he turned the square of red card round and round in his fingers. There was one thin, white piece of cigarette paper left attached. Studer tore it off, held it between his fingers, lit it with a match and let it burn up in the palm of his hand. There was a brief, bright spurt of flame. Studer shone the torch on it. All that was left was a few tiny scraps of black ash. Still, assuming Witschi had used several papers, not all the ash would have disappeared. But the assistant pathologist hadn't mentioned any, and Studer was sure the autopsy had been carried out thoroughly.

He'd have to ring up the Italian again . . . pity it was Sunday.

"You've done well, Schreier, that would never have occurred to me. But will it be enough to convince a jury? And then the gun? It wasn't beside the body. Who picked it up? Got rid of it?"

"Schlumpf, of course," said Schreier. "But don't you think we should go, sergeant? The old woman" — Schreier meant Frau Witschi — "might be back any moment. She closes her kiosk between four and five on a Sunday. It's five past four already . . ."

"Put the door back," said Studer. Schreier picked it up, leant it against the wall and piled up tea-chests and boxes in front of it.

"As long as they don't burn it," Studer sighed. "That would be our evidence gone. Evidence? A nice solid piece of evidence!"

They left the shed and went out through the garden, stopped for a moment at the garden gate and looked back at the house. As they turned to go out into the street they found their way barred by a skinny figure in black.

"Were you looking for me? Or were you looking for something else? On *my* property? Well, Sergeant?"

After every question the voice rose a little higher.

Anastasia Witschi, née Mischler

Studer had only seen Anastasia Witschi briefly, when he arrived in Gerzenstein. There was, in fact, a quite understandable reason why he had almost automatically christened her Anastasia, though it was still odd that that had turned out to be her actual name.

Frau Witschi looked just like a caricature figure personifying censorship. And during the war the French had nicknamed the censor *Anastasie.*

After she had fired off her questions at him, Frau Witschi took a short breather. She surveyed Studer's companion with evident disapproval. And what was that fellow doing here, she asked, in particularly venomous tones, her voice cracking as she spoke. Schreier flushed.

Studer felt ill at ease, but did not show it. His toes were dancing up and down inside his shoes, but no one could see that. "It was you we were looking for, Frau Witschi," he said, his voice slipping into its deepest tones, probably in compensation for the shrillness of the woman's. "We've had a look at your garden. A lovely garden, really, a marvellous garden. It needs a bit of care and attention, but that's understandable, of course."

"You haven't been up here before?" Frau Witschi asked.

Studer looked at her. Was the question a trap? No . . . probably not. So Sonja hadn't told her about his visit. In any case, Frau Witschi did not seem to expect an answer, since she immediately went on to say that if the sergeant had any questions to ask, he should come in. "I've got nothing to hide. No, definitely not. *Our* conscience is clear, which is not something everyone can say."

Now Schreier turned pale, he was trembling. Strange how sensitive these supposedly hard-boiled characters could be . . .

"Keep calm now," Studer said softly, placing his hand on Schreier's shoulder. "You go back. And thank you, you've been a great help. Goodbye."

Silently Schreier shook Studer by the hand. He ignored the woman.

"You're much too good with those people, Herr Studer," Frau Witschi said. ("Herr Studer", not just "sergeant". He was to feel they were two respectable citizens talking to each other.) "Come in, we can't stand out here all day."

The kitchen was clean. No dirty dishes left in the sink. The comb had disappeared from the table. The living-room had been tidied up too.

The vase below the picture of Wendelin Witschi had gone.

"Sit down, Herr Studer. I'll get us something to drink, you'll be thirsty."

She returned with a bottle of raspberry cordial and two glasses. Like it or not, Studer had to join her in a drink. He shuddered slightly.

"My poor husband," said Frau Witschi, sniffing audibly. She wiped her eyes with her handkerchief. But her eyes were dry, and stayed dry.

"True, true," said Studer, putting his hand over his glass that Frau Witschi was about to refill with the sickly concoction. "It was sad that he had to die in that way. But perhaps it was for the best, after all . . ."

"For the best? What do you mean, for the best?"

"Er, well, the insurance . . ." said Studer, taking his time over lighting a Brissago. A torrent of words poured over him. Studer let it bounce off his broad back.

It was strange, almost a vision. The room darkens, quite suddenly. The lamp, with its green shade, is giving off a gloomy light. There are empty plates on the table. Sitting at the head is the late Wendelin Witschi. On his right, his wife, on his left, Sonja, opposite him, his son.

Witschi is silent. Weariness has etched deep lines round his mouth, on his forehead. His wife doesn't stop her chatter. She's moaning. It was his fault, his fault alone. He'd plunged the family into debt, so it was up to him to get them out of it again. He'd borrowed money without asking anyone — and he was the one who'd bought those Kreuger shares, wasn't he? Witschi raises his hand, a skinny white hand, as if he wants to make an objection, but the woman keeps jabbering on. No, no, he was to keep his mouth shut, he was to sit and listen. Then, suddenly, in a whisper: The insurance policies would bring in some money . . . just an accident, nothing serious. But it had to be done so that it looked like an accident. There were enough men around with a criminal record they could put the blame on.

And now the son joins in. His sister's been carrying on with one of them, she should see to it. Arrange a rendezvous with the fellow so he wouldn't have an alibi. Then they could accuse him and when his father said he recognized him, he was the one, the fellow wouldn't be able to do anything about it.

At the head of the table Witschi has clasped his hands. He keeps shaking his head, but no one is paying any attention to him. The flood of words continues. His son takes over from his wife, his wife from his son. Sonja sits there, quietly sobbing into her handkerchief. She has put her hand under her father's left hand, but it's no use, Sonja can find nowhere to hide from the plans of the other two.

How often had that scene been played out, just as Studer visualized it, now, here in the Witschis' living-room, as Anastasia Witschi went on and on at him, her words whistling past his ears like a chill North wind.

Studer nodded, just kept on nodding at the woman's words. It was all lies anyway, so why bother to listen?

He could see the shed quite clearly in his mind's eye. The woman was holding a stable lamp. And Witschi was trying out the gun. He was shooting at the white rectangle where the door had been planed, each time from a distance of four inches. No more and no less. He tried with one cigarette paper, then with three, then with five.

At which point were there no more scorch marks? Fifteen cartridge cases, Studer thought. Where was the box? They ought to find it. And the scene that kept interrupting his reflections: Witschi experimenting with the gun by the light of the stable lamp. His wife must have been holding a sack, to muffle the sound. Otherwise how was it the neighbours hadn't heard anything? Perhaps they had . . . The next house was about fifty yards away. Should he go and ask?

As if emerging from a dream, Studer interrupted Frau Witschi's torrent of words and said quietly, "When your husband was shooting at the door in the shed, did you have a sack to muffle the sound?"

The glass shattered on the floor. Frau Witschi's eyes opened wide, there was a white membrane over one of them. "What? . . . What? . . ." Frau Witschi stammered.

"Nothing, nothing." Wearily Studer waved the question aside. "That's neither here nor there now Schlumpf's confessed." But beneath his half-closed lids Studer was observing the woman's reaction keenly.

A sigh of relief. Frau Witschi got up, went into the kitchen, came back with a dustpan and brush and swept up the broken glass.

"Break a glass, mend your luck." Studer quoted the proverb mechanically.

It brought a venomous look from the woman. Then she said, "So, the murderer's finally confessed, has he? Thank goodness. Then there's nothing more for you to do here, Sergeant" (He smiled. It was no longer "Herr Studer".)

"You're quite right, Frau Witschi, there's nothing more for me to do here."

What time was it? It was still broad daylight outside. The shed was at the bottom of the garden, there was a good view of it through the window. Studer stared at it for a long time. He thought, I'll have to spend the night keeping watch here. Frau Witschi and her son will try to burn the door. Should I have kept my mouth shut?

No, it was all right. Sometimes a warning shot like that was quite effective. Although the case was a hopeless mess anyway. A murky business, murky . . . Commissaire Madelin was right. A murder out in the country! Shall we just let Witschi rest in peace? He sacrificed himself for his family. Shot himself so the insurance will pay out . . . Did he really shoot himself? . . . With his arm stuck out at right angles? Perhaps there is more to this case? But who killed him then? . . . Schlumpf? Schlumpf after all? Can someone commit a murder out of love? . . . Why not? Though it's unlikely . . . Armin, then? The *maquereau*? . . . No, no, he wouldn't have the courage . . . The mother? *Chabis*. Who then? If only he knew who had bought the gun, perhaps that would give him something to work on . . .

"Where does your daughter work in Bern?" he asked out loud.

"At Loeb's." The old woman's voice was shaking. It was time he left Frau Anastasia in peace, Studer thought. He held out his hand to say goodbye, but Frau Witschi did not see it. She was already heading for the door with her tiny steps. She opened it. The smile on her lips was frozen.

"*Auf Wiedersehen*, Herr Studer," she said.

Studer silently bowed his head.

Schwomm

Studer could hear the music while he was still out in the street. The accordion was particularly loud. Schreier must have taken his place with them again.

And who was that sitting at the table in his high collar, black boots and grey flannel trousers, going on and on at Armin Witschi?

Schwomm, the schoolteacher.

He leapt up as Studer walked past. His face had an artless, childlike look. There was a little blond moustache over his upper lip.

"Sergeant," he said breathlessly, "I hear you are looking into the Witschi case. For some time I have been hesitating whether to reveal what I know of the matter to you, but now I feel it is my duty, in the name of Swiss justice, to . . ."

"Oh do stop going on like that, Schwomm," Witschi interrupted rudely. Studer gave him a severe look, but he just nodded, as if to say, You can stare as much as you like, you don't frighten me.

"Why don't you join me at my table, Herr Schwomm?" Studer asked politely, gesturing towards the table where Ellenberger was still sitting, reflectively twirling his wine-glass between his fingers.

Schwomm sat down. That is, he placed himself on the extreme edge of the iron garden chair, then took out his handkerchief and mopped his brow. His face was almost as yellow as his curly hair.

"You see, by chance, on the evening when Witschi

fell victim to that infamous crime," said Schwomm, kneading his palms, "I happened to hear two shots . . ."

"You did?" said Studer dryly.

"Huh!" said Ellenberger, turning down the corners of his mouth.

"Yes." The schoolteacher nodded. "Two shots. By chance I happened to be taking a walk in the woods that evening. With a . . . companion. I don't have to say who was in the woods with me, do I?"

Ellenberger's booming bass laugh made Schwomm even more embarrassed.

"Couldn't I speak with you in private, Sergeant?" he asked, blushing.

Studer shook his head. He was less interested in what the teacher had to tell him than in what he was clearly trying to keep from him. And the man's behaviour gave him a clue as to what he wanted to conceal.

Schwomm cleared his throat. "It was around ten when I left the road and took a path. I wandered lonely as a cloud, as the poet says, without a thought in my mind. It was a still, soft evening, sleepy birds were chirping in the branches . . ."

"Huh!" Ellenberger squawked again, but Studer waved him to keep quiet. Armin Witschi's table was empty. Gerber was dancing with Sonja again, followed by the hostile glances of the Convict Band. The *maquereau* was dancing with the waitress and seemed to be urgently explaining something to her (or perhaps he was trying to persuade her to do something?)

". . . and from time to time some animal scurried off to its den. I and my, er . . . my companion must have penetrated quite deep into the heart of the woods, when I heard the clatter of a motorcycle approaching along the road, a light motorcycle, I might add . . ."

"Add away, add away," said Ellenberger with a hoarse croak. Was it a laugh?

But now Schwomm refused to be distracted. "The noise, if I may call it that, stopped suddenly. I heard twigs cracking . . ."

"Could you give an estimate of the distance, I mean the distance you were from the road?" asked Studer amid a cloud of smoke from his Brissago.

"Not precisely," said Schwomm quietly. He seemed to be in a kind of trance. He was gazing into the distance, though in this case the distance was a packed inn garden. "Perhaps I could find the place where I was again . . ."

"Good," said Studer. "Go on, sir."

"Of course, at that point I didn't pay much attention to the motorcycle approaching and stopping. I only remembered it later, when I heard people in the village talking of a light motorcycle, a Zehnder, being found, the motorcycle that is said to have belonged to the man who had that unfortunate accident, Wendelin Witschi . . . "

Unfortunate accident? Studer thought. Why did the man first of all describe Witschi as the victim of an infamous crime and now of an unfortunate accident? Could he . . .? And he remembered the rudeness with which Armin Witschi had addressed him.

"Go on," he said.

But Schwomm did not need to be prompted. He spoke, accompanying his words with gestures that were clearly supposed to dramatize the scene: "Then, suddenly, in the stillness of the woods, two shots rang out. My companion started. I calmed her . . . him down, telling her . . . him that it wouldn't be anything serious. But since I was afraid . . . or, rather, since my companion was afraid we might be attacked, we left

122

the woods, making a long detour and coming back on to the road well outside the village. After we had been proceeding along it for some time, we saw a motorcycle that had been left by the roadside. It was leant against a tree . . ."

Schwomm paused.

"You didn't see anyone?" Studer asked.

"See? No. Only heard. After the two shots there was the sound of steps. We also noticed a dark shadow, but it wasn't coming towards the road, it was going in the opposite direction, towards the spot where the woods run along the boundary of Herr Ellenberger's tree nursery."

"A shadow?" Studer asked. "Could you give me a description?"

Instead of answering the question, Schwomm asked mildly, "But Schlumpf's confession has tied up the case, hasn't it?"

"Oh, definitely." Studer stared down at his clasped hands. He was listening to the tone of the other man's voice. Why had the schoolteacher started to make a statement, only to break off before he had finished to ask if the case wasn't closed?

There were two possibilities: either Schwomm wanted to push himself forward so he could play a role in the trial — and that possibility was very likely anyway — or he knew something but for some reason or other didn't dare come out with the truth, so he was soothing his conscience by telling Studer half of what he knew. It was surely not for nothing that an educated man — he was a secondary-school teacher, after all — would indulge in such tediously flowery speech. Sleepy birds were chirping in the branches indeed! Then there was the expression that he had probably let slip unintentionally: the unfortunate accident.

The men at the table were silent. The band stopped. The piece was over and the hum of voices immediately increased in volume. As the three from the next table returned to their seats, Sonja gave the teacher an uninterested glance. She hadn't been Schwomm's "companion" then, if looks meant anything. Armin's face, on the other hand, was twisted in a slight frown. He seemed to be looking for someone. Sometimes his eye would light briefly on the schoolteacher, then wander off round the garden again, searching, eventually fixing on the door into the inn.

The waitress was standing there. Studer sensed more than he actually saw her unobtrusive sign, a slight movement of the head, a twitch at the corner of the mouth. Armin leant back, yawned and put his hand over his mouth. An almost imperceptible nod. The yawn was presumably just an attempt to distract any observers from the movement of his head.

Studer's tiredness had vanished. He felt he was no longer shut out, he was in the middle of the events. Above all, something seemed to be going on, something was about to happen, he could feel it in his bones. He kept calm. First of all he had to get as much as he could out of this schoolteacher with the sponge on top, and then . . .

Studer already had his programme for the next day worked out. But a lot could happen between one day and the next . . . There was the whole of the night between them. And he knew he wasn't going to get much sleep in the night to come. But what did that matter? There was a job of work to be done. However tangled and confused the business might seem, it was his job to get things straightened out. That's what the police were there for.

"And what did this shadow look like?" The teacher

had been daydreaming and Studer ambushed him with his question. Schwomm came to with a start.

"It scurried" (Scurried! There was another of those words again), "it scurried past about thirty feet away from us . . . er . . . from me. How tall? Medium height . . . yes, medium height . . ." Suddenly Schwomm fell silent again.

"Medium height?" Studer asked in friendly tones. "What I really need is some comparison. About how tall was it, this shadow? Between you and me, Herr Schwomm, this shadow might perhaps not be important at all, but it might possibly confirm our suspicions. If it was the same height as, say, the accused, it would be very important for the judges, who of course give no credence to a confession until all the accused's movements before and after the deed have been established, as well as the whole psychological motivation."

"I've not really seen Erwin Schlumpf that often . . . but I would say the shadow was about his height."

"It would be extremely helpful for us if we could perhaps hear the opinion of the . . . the person you were with, though that will probably not be possible. . ."

"Out of the question, completely out of the question. I couldn't take it upon myself . . ."

"All right." Studer cut short his protestations. He squinted across at Armin's table. Something seemed to be going on. He was whispering urgently to his sister and had stretched out a hand to stop Gerber listening to what he was saying. Then Armin stood up. The waitress was still leaning against the post of the door to the bar. She seemed to have suddenly gone deaf, and blind as well, since she wasn't responding to the calls or waves of her customers. But she did see Armin stand up, and she turned round and disappeared into the interior of the Bear. Armin ambled across the garden, head bowed. Suddenly he accelerated. A couple of long strides and he was swallowed up in the open doorway.

"All right," Studer repeated after a pause. He couldn't take his eyes off Sonja. Her girlish features were agitated by bewilderment, fear, despair.

"If only she would trust me," Studer thought. As he absentmindedly listened to what Schwomm had to say next, his mind was on his wife. If she were here . . . Since he'd weaned her off novels, Hedy (Frau Studer was called Hedwig) had proved very good at getting worried, reticent people — especially women — to speak.

What Schwomm was saying was, "Of course I'm not claiming to have seen Schlumpf fleeing from the scene of his infamous crime. (Infamous crime — unfortunate accident, went through Studer's mind.) But it certainly struck me as odd that the shadow should be running towards Herr Ellenberger's tree nursery . . ."

"My tree nursery as the realm of shadows, heheheh," Ellenberger sniggered. Studer silenced him with a glance.

"And you are quite sure you heard two shots, and that after the two shots you saw the shadow go off in the direction of the tree nursery?"

"I believe," Schwomm stammered, "I believe I heard two shots." He looked round, as if in search of help, avoiding looking Studer in the eye.

"Believe! Believe!" said Studer reproachfully. "A man like you shouldn't believe, he should be certain. So two shots, then? Yes?"

"Yeees." It sounded like a sigh.

Silence. Then the band struck up again. "If you should give your heart away" of all songs. Studer saw Gerber ask Sonja to dance. She shook her head, grabbed her little handbag and dashed out through the garden. Was she running away? Or was it a last desperate attempt to catch up with someone?

"Who was it who told you to give me this story of two shots when I have five witnesses ready to testify that there was only one?" (The five witnesses were pure invention, there was nothing of the sort in Murmann's file. The things one had to do to get at the truth!)

"Five witnesses?" Schwomm had gone pale. "Testify?"

"Yes, testify, " said Studer tersely. "But I'm not interested in all that. You have something on your conscience, Herr Schwomm, and you've tried to relieve it by telling me just half — what am I saying? Half? — by telling me a quarter of the truth. I've heard enough." Schwomm opened his mouth to justify himself, but Studer waved his explanations away. "I don't believe anything you say any more. Now if you will excuse me, I have to go."

When Studer spoke formal German instead of dialect, which happened seldom enough, it always produced the same effect. Whether members of the public or young detectives, they all felt it was best to give the sergeant a wide berth.

"You're getting hot, very hot," croaked Ellenberger. "*Vous brûlez, Commissaire.*" He was referring to the game where you have to find some hidden object and those in the know guide you by telling you how cold, warm, warmer, hot, you're getting.

"There'll come a time when you have to stop playing games too, Herr Ellenberger," Studer said. His face was pale, his fists clenched. Then he shrugged his shoulders and made his way between the noisy tables to the door through which Armin Witschi had vanished.

The band had moved on to a folk song played as a one-step:

Muss i denn, muss i denn zum Städtle hinaus . . .

Love in the dock

Monday morning, seven thirty, Corporal Murmann's office.

Studer was sitting at the window looking out into the garden. It was drizzling and it was cool. The warm Sunday had been a delusion.

Sergeant Studer was alone. He looked tired. He was hunched up in the comfortable armchair in his favourite posture, forearms on his thighs, hands clasped. The skin on his face had the look of sodden paper. From time to time he sighed.

In his hand he had a letter, three closely written sheets. He read a few lines, put the letter down, lifted it up again, shook his head. It was from Münch, the lawyer he played billiards with, who had strange things to relate, things that might . . . that might contain the solution, the solution to the baffling Witschi case. "Highly confidential" was written across the top. What did Münch think he was doing? Telling him interesting facts and not allowing him to use them?

The letter was about acceptances — IOUs to the ordinary citizen, thought Studer — which amounted to a considerable sum. Bills of exchange, that is, which had been accepted by a "person living in Gerzenstein" and were now awaiting payment. A week ago the "person living in Gerzenstein" had come to an agreement with the Cantonal Bank. The bills fell due that very day but, with great reluctance, the bank had agreed to an extension (prolongation was the word the lawyer used) of a week. So they would have to be paid in a week's time. Ten thousand francs. A tidy sum. Münch did not give the name of the person who had accepted them, but it was not difficult to guess. And it was Witschi who had pocketed the money. Six months ago . . .

That Witschi must have been a fly customer, and he must have got through a great deal of money. What had he done with it? Indulged in speculation? Perhaps. Münch said that Witschi was close to bankruptcy (and, funnily enough, so was the "person from Gerzenstein"). The lawyer had an odd story to tell. He went on:

Besides that, sergeant, I have a strange story for you. You will remember I told you, that time we saw Ellenberger when we were playing billiards, that Ellenberger had been to see me to call in a second mortgage he had on Wendelin Witschi's house. Well that wasn't exactly the case. Ellenberger had already been to see me, a week before, and he brought an IOU for fifteen thousand francs he had from Witschi. As security Witschi had deposited with him a life insurance policy for twenty thousand francs. Ellenberger had agreed to keep up the premiums. Now Ellenberger wanted to withdraw from the agreement, why I don't know. He was demanding repayment of the loan, plus the insurance premiums, and he wanted me to communicate that to Witschi. I telephoned Gerzenstein on Monday afternoon (May 1, that was), asking Witschi to come and see me at my office. He arrived at about five and I informed him of Ellenberger's decision. Witschi got very worked up, said he was ruined and there was nothing left for it but to do away with himself. I pointed out that that would not change things, indeed, it would make matters worse, since in that case the insurance company would refuse to pay out on the policy.

There followed a certain amount of legalese, after which Münch continued:

Witschi started to moan. He went on and on about his wife and his son, who were making life hell for him, as he put it. I tried to calm him down, but he got more and more worked up. Suddenly he took a gun out of his pocket and threatened to shoot himself there and then, in my office, if I refused to help him. The man was beginning to get on my nerves. I wanted to get rid of him, but he just went on whining and moaning. The mayor was going to have him put away, he said, and ... I cut him short. I told him that was none of my business and he should see that he got out of my office, I could do without all the carry-on. At that he started to cry and said he wouldn't go until he had been given advice. But I had no advice to give him, and told him so. Then he'd shoot himself, Witschi said. Not in my office, I said, he wouldn't have the necessary peace and quiet. But I did have an small, empty room, I added, and if he cared to go there, he would have the ideal opportunity to blow his brains out. You'll be thinking I'm a heartless beast, sergeant, but I'm not. You must remember that in my practice as a lawyer I have had many similar cases. Threatening suicide is an easy way to put pressure on others. These people don't intend to commit suicide, they're just seeking attention and trying to get something out of you. I'm telling you all this in confidence, as I'm sure you'll understand.

Studer shook his head. Was it a genuine case of despair after all? In his mind's eye he saw Witschi lying on the table in the bright, all-too-white room of the Institute for Forensic Medicine ... with the calm expression of a man released from torment.

The rest of Münch's letter seemed to confirm the lawyer's opinion of threatened suicides:

130

I took Witschi to a quiet little room, said, 'Be my guest,' and closed the door. I hadn't taken more than five steps when I heard a shot. Now I did feel a bit uneasy. I went back and opened the door. Witschi was standing there in the middle of the room. It was an old mirror hanging on the wall that had been on the receiving end. But Witschi had spared himself. What strikes me as odd is that he should be found in the woods two days later with a bullet through his head. Of course, I can't express an opinion . . .

The door opened and two women came in. Frau Murmann, tall, motherly, protective, led Sonja into the room.

Studer looked at them. He nodded. "Thank you, Frau Murmann," he said. "There was no fuss?"

"None whatsoever," replied Frau Murmann. "I waited for her at the station and she was quite happy to come along with me."

"We're going to go to Thun together, Sonja, to visit Schlumpf. Is that all right by you? It was just that I didn't want your mother to know, that's why I sent Frau Murmann to tell you. You do understand? That's all there is to it."

"Yes, Sergeant." Sonja nodded earnestly.

"But the people here don't have to see us," Studer went on. "Murmann's lending me his motorbike, he'll take it out of the village and wait for us. You'll go on ahead and we'll meet there. You'll be on the pillion and we'll be in Thun by nine. Go with Frau Murmann for the moment, I still have some work to do. I'll tell you when we're leaving. Have you got all that?"

Sonja said nothing, just nodded.

"Come along, lassie," said Frau Murmann.

But Sonja hesitated. Finally she managed to stammer out a question (Studer could tell the words had to force their way out through the sobs stuck in her throat): Did the sergeant know where Armin was?

"Oh? Isn't he at home?"

"No, he's been gone since . . . well, since he left the table in the garden of the Bear. Mother doesn't seem worried, she's gone to the kiosk as usual this morning. What do you think, sergeant?"

The sergeant didn't seem to think anything, he remained silent. He'd expected something like this. He'd spent the whole night in the Witschis' garden, hiding behind a large hazel bush, never taking his eyes off the shed. Before starting his watch he had gone into the shed. The door with the marks from Witschi's shooting practice (actually, he'd thought to himself, there's nothing to prove it was Witschi who'd been practising) was still in the same place and no one tried to take it away during the night. All was quiet and dark in the house. Frau Anastasia had come home at ten o'clock, for an hour there'd been a light on in the kitchen, then all had been dark again until the morning. Studer was convinced Frau Witschi knew where her son had gone. He was sure to turn up again, once the coast was clear.

But what was it that had driven Armin Witschi, the *maquereau*, away? Could it have been the words Schreier had spoken out loud: "Aha, so Schlumpfli's confessed, has he?"

Could it be that Schlumpf's confession was not part of the plan?

Studer could easily have found out where Armin had gone. But for the moment he didn't want to know. At breakfast that morning Berta, the waitress, had obviously been crying. She kept sniffing now and then and Studer had asked in sympathetic tones what was wrong?

Nothing, nothing was wrong, Berta had replied.

At that Studer had not been able to control himself and had asked in the same sympathetic tones how much money she had had to give to Armin Witschi?

Five hundred francs, everything she'd saved up! she exclaimed. But the sergeant must keep it to himself, she went on, he mustn't tell anyone. As soon as the insurance had paid out on the policies Armin was going to marry her, he'd promised, yes, he'd sworn he would. She didn't know why she was telling the sergeant all this, she wasn't supposed to say anything, Armin had made her promise — and so on and so on.

Studer had patted the girl's hand comfortingly. God, didn't people have a hard time of it here on earth! This poor waitress. She wasn't in the first flush of youth, had to be nice to the customers all the time, had to listen to crude jokes, put up with being pawed and mauled. Then along came someone like Armin Witschi, friendly, considerate, unhappy, educated . . . Was it surprising the girl should fall in love with him? Perhaps Armin wasn't such a bad lot after all? He ought to have a word with him some time, Studer thought, with a mental grin at himself: Sergeant Studer as matchmaker!

Sonja was waiting for an answer. She was looking expectantly at Studer. "Armin'll be back," he said. "Go along with Frau Murmann now. We'll be leaving in an hour."

So Sonja went.

Studer sat down at the desk. He took a large sheet of paper, placed it in front of him and wrote at the top, in the middle of the sheet,

SUMMARY OF THE FACTS

Then he started to think. But that was as far as he got. One of the chief characteristics of the Witschi case seemed to be that it was impossible to get any single part of it finished off. Hadn't he intended to observe the behaviour of Ellenberger and the mayor while they were playing Jass? What had stopped him? The telephone, of course, and Schreier's revelation.

And now, of course, the telephone rang. Studer lifted the receiver and said, as he did in his office in Bern, "Yes?"

"Is that you, Studer?" a voice asked. It was his captain.

"Yes," said Studer. "What is it?"

"Right, listen. This morning Reinhardt went round the gunsmiths. Before they were open, even. And he struck lucky at the very first one. The owner was there already and he remembered selling a Browning a fortnight ago. The same type, the same number. He remembered the man who bought it . . ."

"And?" Studer asked, since the captain did not continue.

"Getting impatient, eh? Keep your hair on, Studer. You'll end up with egg all over your face again . . . Eh? . . . You've gone quiet, Studer. Well then, Reinhardt told me the gunsmith remembered the purchaser well. It was an old man, with no teeth left. He had on a linen suit, and the gunsmith noticed the man was wearing black silk socks with brown shoes. He didn't say what his name was . . ."

"That doesn't matter." Studer's voice was slightly hesitant. On the one hand it was hard to digest the information, on the other, he had expected something like this.

"Listen, Captain," said Studer, "I'm sending you a Browning, I'll send it express delivery. And Forensic will send you the bullet they took out of Witschi's skull. Have you an expert on hand? Yes? Good. Give them to him and get him to write a report on whether the bullet came from the gun I'm sending. And get Reinhardt to go round the other gunsmiths as well. It could be another gun of the same make has been sold. Understood? And I need that report this evening. By five at the latest. Bye."

Studer replaced the receiver carefully and rested his cheek on his fist. As he did so, the words SUMMARY OF THE FACTS neatly written at the top of the sheet of paper caught his eye. That can wait, he thought to himself, crossed them out, folded the paper precisely and put it in his jacket pocket.

* * *

Wet socks are unpleasant. Especially when you have the feeling the cold that started two days ago is about to go down on to your chest. After all, when you reach a certain age you get more susceptible to illness, you worry about your health more, you're afraid of catching pneumonia, you'd like a change of dry clothes to avoid the danger. But if that's not possible (you can't just ask an elegant examining magistrate in his silk shirt, "Can you lend me a pair of dry socks?") then you have to grit your teeth, even if your teeth have ideas of their own and seem determined to make a chattering noise . . .

That was what you got when you insisted on hopping on a bike like a twenty-year-old and driving fifteen miles in the pouring rain. And it was no comfort that Sonja's stockings were wet through as well.

The said Sonja was waiting out in the corridor. A tiny figure huddled up on a wooden bench. A policeman was patrolling up and down

Once more Studer was sitting on the chair that was too small for him, the chair that was most certainly intended for suspects, was sitting facing the examining magistrate, who twisted the signet ring with the coat of arms round and round as he spoke:

"I don't understand you, Herr Studer. The matter has been cleared up. We have the man's confession, it's complete, he states that . . . he states that . . ." The magistrate stopped fiddling with his ring and rummaged nervously round among the papers on his desk. Eventually the blue cardboard folder appeared with the label which said:

Schlumpf, Erwin:
MURDER

"He states that . . ." the examining magistrate said for the third time, struggling with the recalcitrant pages, "ah, here we have it: 'I lay in wait for Herr Witschi and forced him to dismount at gun-point. We proceeded into the woods, where I forced him to hand over his wallet, and his watch and purse as well. What my motivation was for shooting him afterwards I could not say. I think I was afraid he might have recognized me, although I had wrapped a black scarf round the lower half of my face. (In response to questioning) I needed money to buy a bicycle —' "

The examining magistrate halted. Studer had blown his nose, producing a veritable trumpet fanfare. When he stopped, he sneezed, but the sneeze sounded like suppressed giggling. Finally he had himself under control again and asked, his eyes streaming, "Are those Schlumpfli's own words? I mean things like 'We proceeded into the woods' and 'What my motivation was I could not say.' Did he really say that?"

The examining magistrate was offended. "You yourself know, sergeant," he said in a severe voice, "that we are responsible for formulating statements. We can't have someone taking all the ramblings of an accused person down in shorthand. Just think how huge the files would be."

"Well now, you see, sir, I have always thought that was a big mistake. I wouldn't just have the statements of witnesses and accused taken down in shorthand, I'd have them recorded on discs. Then you'd be able to hear the tone of voice . . ."

Silence. It looked as if the examining magistrate was still in a huff. Studer decided on a placatory approach. He got up and went over to the fireplace in the corner of the room. There was a wood fire flickering in the grate — in May! He stood with his back to it and warmed the soles of his shoes.

"The fact is, sir, some of the odd details about this case have been confirmed and they make it difficult for me to believe Schlumpf is guilty. I've brought a witness I would like to confront the accused with. Waiting outside in the corridor. But they mustn't see each other for the moment. Have you a room where my witness could wait until called? I'll do that when the time is right."

The examining magistrate nodded. He pressed a button and, when the policeman entered, ordered him to take the person who had come with the sergeant to the waiting room (just like at the dentist's, Studer thought) and then bring up Erwin Schlumpf.

Schlumpf's first words were, "But I've confessed. What more do you want?"

Only then did he notice Studer. He gave him a nod, hardly raising his eyes from the floor, and tried to slip across to the chair. But Studer strode over to meet him, hand outstretched.

"How've you been since I saw you last, Schlumpfli," he said.

"Not very well, Sergeant," Schlumpf said, his hand hanging lifelessly in Studer's. Studer gave the limp hand a squeeze.

"You've changed your mind, Schlumpfli, or so I've heard?"

"Yes. It was weighing too heavily on my conscience."

"Huh!" said Studer with a smile. Schlumpf gave him a surprised look.

"Don't you believe me, Sergeant?"

"I still believe what you told me on the train." Studer sneezed.

"*Gesundheit*," Schlumpf said automatically. He was sitting on the defendant's chair with his head bowed. From time to time he squinted across at Studer, as if that was where the danger was coming from. He looked like a schoolboy who suspects a box round the ears is on its way and wants to make sure he sees it coming so he can block it with his elbows.

"I'm not going to hurt you, Schlumpfli," Studer said, "I just want to help you. Did you know the man who was brought in yesterday for stealing a car?"

It made Schlumpf start. His eyes opened wide, his mouth too. He was about to speak when the examining magistrate broke in.

"What's all this about, Studer?"

"Nothing, sir. Schlumpf's given me the answer already." After a short pause, he asked, "It's all right if I smoke, is it?" and took a yellow packet out of his pocket. With a grin: "A cigarette. And I'm sure Schlumpf would like one. It'll clear the air."

The examining magistrate could not repress a smile. A queer customer, this Studer . . .

There was a chair standing by itself in a corner. Studer picked it up by the backrest, swung it round so it was in the middle of the room, sat astride it, leant his

138

forearms on the backrest and, looking Schlumpf straight in the eye, said:

"Why did you give the examining magistrate this cock-and-bull story? It's just a load of rubbish. The way you killed Witschi was quite different. You got him to stop, that much could well be true, but then you told him someone wanted to speak to him and as he walked in front of you, you shot him. Then you turned the body over and took out his wallet. Isn't that the way it was? You left the corpse lying on its back, didn't you? Now's the time to tell the truth. It's no use lying, I know what happened."

"Yes, Sergeant. He was lying on his back, the moon was shining and Witschi was staring at me . . . I ran and ran . . ."

Studer stood up and threw out his hand like a circus artiste. "Q. E. D. There's your proof."

With two steps he was at the table leafing through the file. He pulled out a photograph and stuck it in front of Schlumpf's nose.

"That's the way Witschi was lying, on his front, you blockhead. And he can't have been on his back at all because there are no pine needles on his jacket. Do you see?"

Turning to the magistrate, he said, "Isn't there another photo there. One with just the head?"

The magistrate was somewhat disconcerted. He hunted through the file. Yes, there was another photograph, he was sure of that. Two with the whole body and one with just the head, the head with the bullet hole behind the right ear and the ground strewn with pine needles. Eventually he found it and handed it to Studer.

"The magnifying glass," said Studer. It sounded like a command.

"Here, Herr Studer." The examining magistrate was getting worried. How much longer was he going to have to put up with being ordered around by this detective?

Studer went over to the window. It had gone quiet in the room. The rain was drumming monotonously against the window-panes. Studer stared through the magnifying glass, stared and stared. Finally he said, "I need to have this enlarged. May I take it?"

"That is really a matter for the examining magistrate's office," said the magistrate, trying to make it sound like a matter-of-fact refusal.

"Yes, and then it'll take three weeks. I have a man available who can get it done for this evening . . . So I can have it, then?" Studer took an envelope from the table, tore off a sheet of paper from the block, scribbled a few words on it, sealed the envelope and pressed the buzzer. By the time the policeman outside opened the door, Studer was already waiting for him.

"Get on your bike and take this to the station, send it express. Here's the money, but be quick about it."

The policeman gave the examining magistrate an astonished look. The latter, slightly embarrassed, nodded. Then he said, "But first of all bring in the person who came with the sergeant. You seem to have forgotten about that, Herr Studer?"

"You're right," said Studer abstractedly, "I'd quite forgotten about that." He rubbed his forehead and massaged his eyelids with thumb and index finger.

Those black dots on the pine needles next to the head . . . What might those black dots mean? They looked as if they could be tiny scraps of burnt cigarette paper. And if they were recognizable as such on the enlargement . . . Difficult, but not impossible . . . And then . . . Then Schwomm might not have been lying

140

when he spoke of two shots . . . That would make the affair considerably easier to sort out . . . dead easy . . .

A shrill little cry. Sonja was in the doorway.

Schlumpf leapt up.

"Go on, you can shake hands," said Studer dryly from the corner.

They stood facing each other, blushing, embarrassed, arms hanging down.

Finally: "Hello, Erwin."

The reply, choking: "Hello, Sonja."

"Take a seat," said Studer, placing his chair close to Schlumpf's. Sonja thanked Studer with a nod and sat down. She laid her tiny hand with the not-quite-clean fingernails on Schlumpf's arm and repeated, very quietly, "Hello, Erwin. How are you?"

Schlumpf said nothing. Studer was in front of the fireplace again, warming the backs of his legs and looking at the pair. The magistrate gave him a questioning look, but Studer waved him away. Let things take their course. He even placed his finger to his lips in an exaggerated gesture.

A gust of wind made the window-panes rattle slightly. Then the monotonous pitter-patter of the rain again. Another gust came down the chimney and Studer was engulfed in a blue cloud. He really needed to cough, but he suppressed the urge. He didn't want to break the silence.

Sonja's hand stroked Schlumpf's sleeve, up and down, stopped on his wrist and stayed there.

"You're a good boy," Sonja said softly. Her eyes were wide and fixed on her friend's. And Schlumpf, too, just looked and looked. Studer hardly recognized his face. It wasn't a smiling face, it was calm and very serious. It genuinely looked as if Schlumpf had suddenly grown up.

"Was it very hard?" Sonja asked softly. They both seemed to have forgotten that they were not alone in the room. Suddenly Schlumpf gave a deep sigh and the upper part of his body slumped forward. His head was in the girl's lap. Little Sonja seemed to grow. She was sitting up straight, her hands clasped over Schlumpf's head.

"Yes, you're a good boy. I was thinking of you all the time, you know that, don't you. Thinking of you all the time."

It sounded like a lullaby.

The words came haltingly, scarcely comprehensible, for Schlumpf left his head in Sonja's lap and her dress muffled them. "I did it for you."

Then his head came up. Schlumpf was smiling now, even if it was a strangely forced smile. "I'm used to this kind of thing, you know."

Although he had lifted up his head, Sonja's hands were still clasped round his neck. She drew him closer, kissed him on the forehead.

"You mustn't think about that any more. Eh? Not any more, that's all in the past."

Schlumpf nodded earnestly.

Studer coughed. He couldn't hold it back any longer, otherwise the smoke would have settled on his lungs. His nose-blowing produced a trumpet fanfare again, but a triumphant one. The expression on the face of the examining magistrate had softened. He was playing with a paper-knife, softly drumming on the folder, on which was written: "Schlumpf, Erwin" in beautifully neat handwriting and underneath it, in block capitals: "MURDER". He softly put the paper-knife down and tapped the bottom of the file on the desk-top. Then he picked up the fat volume that was lying at the side of his desk, shoved the file underneath it and patted the cover of the book several times.

"Yes," he said, and it was a sigh. He was a bachelor, shy probably. Perhaps he envied young Schlumpf. "Yes," he said again, a bit more firmly this time. "And what does all this mean, Herr Studer?"

"Oh, nothing special," Studer said. "Sonja Witschi would like to make a statement."

That was certainly an exaggeration. Sonja Witschi had steadfastly refused to make a statement. She had maintained a stony silence.

"Fräulein Witschi," said the examining magistrate in his politest tones, "I'll call my clerk immediately, then you can tell us if there is any information you can give us regarding your father's demise." He didn't look up, inwardly annoyed at the pompous way he'd expressed himself.

Studer broke in. He'd be happy to act as clerk, he said. That way they'd all feel more comfortable. And he was quite good with a typewriter, if necessary. Only two fingers, but that should do, if Sonja didn't speak too quickly. The magistrate nodded. Schlumpf had to get up. He stood by the wall, staring at Sonja. And Sonja began to tell her story.

Investments, IOUs and insurance

Ellenberger was behind everything . . .

"He owns the tree nursery in Gerzenstein," Studer interjected.

"How do you know?" the magistrate asked Sonja.

"Father told me. Two weeks ago, I remember it perfectly. We were out for a walk, just the two of us, it was a Sunday, the weather was nice. We went through the woods. Father said he couldn't stand it at home any longer, mother was going on at him all the time, Armin as well, about the insurance policy he'd given as security for a loan. And that was when Father said Ellenberger was behind everything. He was always stirring mother up against him."

"Insurance policy?" the magistrate asked.

"You know, all those little magazines," Studer said, as if that explained everything. "And?"

"We had an accident and life insurance policy as well . . ."

Studer broke in again. "And that had been given to Ellenberger as security for a loan of fifteen thousand francs, hadn't it?"

Sonja nodded.

"That was two years ago," she said. "That's when it all started. Mother's money was invested in foreign shares. I can't remember what they were called, but we got a lot of money from them . . ."

"Dividends." The magistrate nodded.

"Yes. And then suddenly they were worthless and

that was when Father took his life insurance policy and used it as security for a loan from Ellenberger.

"At that time Father went round with Herr Schwomm, the teacher, a lot. Herr Schwomm had a relative in Alsace, who worked for a firm, a German company, that was promising ten percent interest. Yes, I think that was it. Father was so happy. He said now we could get back the money we'd lost and went to Ellenberger for a loan against the insurance policy. Herr Schwomm's relative just took the money and went off to Germany with it and we never saw any of it again. He was arrested in Basel. He'd tricked people in the towns as well, not just in Gerzenstein. The company did exist, in Germany, but he had nothing to do with it. Herr Schwomm asked Father not to say anything about it and father kept his mouth shut."

"I don't think we need put this story in the statement, Herr Studer," the magistrate said.

"Of course not," Studer replied, pressed the shift key a few times and clasped his hands.

"Then things started going from bad to worse," Sonja continued. "It was hardly bearable at home. No money, lots of debts. Armin, who'd had to give up university, getting more and more bitter every day, Mother moaning morning, noon and night . . . Uncle Aeschbacher used to come to see us a lot then. He's a funny man . . . He could be very nice, could Uncle Aeschbacher. I liked him almost as much as Father. When he saw how sad I was getting, he found me the job in Bern. And mother got the newsagent's kiosk. Uncle didn't get on well with father. I don't know why. Father kept watching him, secretly; sometimes I was afraid. Who for? I couldn't say . . . He's a funny man, is Uncle Aeschbacher . . ." Sonja repeated, then fell silent for a moment.

"Uncle Aeschbacher usually came in the evening. I'd be alone in the house then. Mother had to stay in the kiosk until the last train, at nine o'clock, Father came home late as well and Armin . . . You couldn't do anything right for Armin."

Silence. The strong wind outside had died down. The light in the room was grey.

"The other people in the village never knew," said Sonja, her voice very low, "but Uncle Aeschbacher was unhappy. I knew. And I liked him, even though he couldn't stand Father. And Father too . . ."

"That's all well and good," said the examining magistrate, his growing impatience almost palpable, "but what I'm interested in is what happened on the evening of the murder."

Sonja raised her eyes and gave the magistrate a reproachful look. Then she said, in a voice which sounded very much like that of her mother, "I have to tell you about what happened before or you won't be able to follow the rest."

"Of course you must," said Studer. "Just let her tell her story, we've plenty of time. Cigarette, Schlumpfli?"

Schlumpf nodded. Sonja continued her story.

"Six months ago things changed between father and Uncle Aeschbacher. It looked as if my uncle was afraid of father. That was . . ." Sonja halted. "That was after one evening . . ." Sonja blushed and glanced at Schlumpf out of the corner of her eye. He was standing erect, smoking in silence, visibly worked up and inhaling deeply.

"One evening I was alone with Uncle Aeschbacher. He was sad. It was the beginning of December and dark outside. I was going to light the lamp, but Uncle Aeschbacher said, "Leave the lamp, lassie, my eyes are sore." He was silent for a while and held his

146

big hand like a shield over his eyes. I was sitting at the table. "Everything's going wrong," he said. "They didn't appoint me to the Commission." Which Commission? I asked. "Oh, you wouldn't understand," he said. "Come over here a minute." He was sitting in a deep armchair, in a dark corner. I went to him. He sat me on his knee and held me tight. I wasn't afraid, Uncle Aeschbacher was always nice to me."

A sigh.

"Then suddenly the door burst open and the light was switched on. Father and Armin were standing in the doorway. 'Aha,' said Father, 'so I've caught you at last, have I, Aeschbacher? What do you think you're doing, cuddling my daughter?' Uncle pushed me away and jumped up. 'You're sozzled, Witschi,' he said. Then he told me to go away and I didn't hear any more. They spent about an hour together. Armin was there too. From then on Uncle Aeschbacher hardly spoke to me at all any more. But things got worse and worse with Father. Ellenberger gave him some certificates, bills, bonds or something, which he cashed in Bern. Then Father kept disappearing for a week or two and would come back to Gerzenstein tired and sad. When I asked him where he'd been, he just said, 'In Geneva'. Once I saw him by chance in Bern. At the main post office, I had an urgent package from work to post. He didn't see me. He was at a post box, taking out letters, tearing them open then throwing them away. He looked sad. When he walked out of the building he looked like an old man. I picked up one of the envelopes he'd thrown away. It was from a bank in Geneva."

"Speculation and more speculation . . ." said Studer quietly and the magistrate nodded.

It was excusable, what Witschi had done, Studer thought. He'd done it for his family. Wanted to get the money back, his wife's money . . .

But Sonja was continuing:

"He went to see Ellenberger more and more. He was also drinking a lot, Father was. Not all the time. But every week he'd come home drunk once or twice. Once I had to go and buy some schnapps for him. A half litre. He went up to his room early. Mother was out that evening, she'd been invited to Uncle Aeschbacher's and didn't get back till late. The next morning the bottle was empty. I threw it away so mother wouldn't see it."

More silence. You could see the examining magistrate was getting impatient again, but Studer calmed him down with a soothing gesture.

"A week ago today I came home as usual at half past six. Father was already back. He was in the living room, by the piano, and didn't hear me come in. I watched what he was doing. He picked up the vase that's always on the piano and shook it — there was a rattling noise — then he put it back and rearranged the autumn foliage in it. "What are you doing, Father?" I asked. He gave a little start. I didn't repeat my question, but next morning I was first up. There were fifteen cartridge cases in the vase. Really!"

Sonja looked at the magistrate, at Schlumpf. She obviously expected loud exclamations of astonishment, but the two of them remained silent. Studer, sitting at the typewriter, on which he hadn't typed a single word, made a dismissive gesture.

"We know that. And we found the door your father used for target practice."

At this the examining magistrate's curiosity was finally aroused. Studer had to tell him about his discovery in the dingy shed, about the rectangle planed clean on the age-blackened door and about the bullet holes which had no powder traces round them.

The magistrate nodded. "And what happened on Tuesday evening, what were you doing then, Fräulein Witschi?"

"I went for a walk with Erwin," said Sonja, her face still pale. "We were in the woods together, it was a nice evening. I got home about eleven. Father wasn't back. Mother was sitting at the table in the kitchen. She seemed agitated. Armin wasn't home either. I asked where they were, but Mother just shrugged her shoulders. 'Out,' was all she said. Armin got back at half past eleven. Mother asked him, 'Did he . . .?' Armin nodded and started to empty out his pockets."

"Stop," the examining magistrate cried. "Take this down please, Herr Studer." After the usual introductory phrases, he dictated what Sonja had just told them.

"Continue," he said. "The contents of his pockets?"

"A gun, a wallet, a fountain pen, a purse, a watch. Armin put them all on the table. I was so frightened of what might have happened, I couldn't stop trembling. I kept on asking, 'What's happened to Father?' but they didn't answer. Armin opened the wallet and took out one hundred-franc and one fifty-franc note. Mother took them, went to her desk, put the fifty away and came back with three hundreds. Armin took the money, put it on the table and said, 'Right, now listen to me, tomorrow you're to do exactly what I tell you. Father's shot himself.' I cried, 'No!' and started sobbing, 'No, it's not true!' — 'Stop snivelling and listen to me. Father decided it was best for him. But he arranged with us, with mother and me, that it wouldn't look like suicide. If it is suicide, the insurance won't pay out.' I was crying. Then I said, 'But people will realize he shot himself. They can do that in a novel, but not in real life.' I was right, wasn't I, Sergeant?"

"Hmm, yes, perhaps . . ." Studer murmured, fiddling with the sheet of paper in the typewriter. It wasn't aligned properly.

"I told Armin that and I asked him how he could have the heart to let Father kill himself for us. He said the arrangement was that father would just wound himself, seriously enough for the insurance to pay out for total disability — shoot himself in the leg, for example, my brother said, but so that it would have to be amputated . . . My brother said that . . ."

"What a crazy, idiotic, hare-brained idea," the magistrate whispered, stretching out his arms so that his sleeves rucked up almost to his elbows and waving his hands in the air. "That's . . . that's . . . What do you say, Studer?"

"Locard, Dr Locard from Lyons — you know who I mean, sir — writes in one of his books — it was a favourite passage of my friend, Commissaire Madelin, he used to quote it all the time — well, Dr Locard writes that it is a mistake to believe there are normal people. Everyone is at least half mad and any investigation has to take that into account. Perhaps you remember the case of that dental technician in Austria? Put his leg on a chopping block and hacked away at it until it was left hanging by a scrap of flesh, just to pocket a huge sum from the insurance. There was a big trial."

"Well yes," the examining magistrate said, "in Austria. But we're in Switzerland here."

"People are the same everywhere," Studer sighed. "What am I to write?"

The magistrate dictated, haltingly, and his sentences got so tangled Studer had difficulty sorting out the syntax.

"Go on, go on, Fräulein Witschi." The examining magistrate mopped his brow with a small, brightly coloured handkerchief. A faint whiff of lavender wafted through the room.

Sonja was cowed. She didn't understand what all this was about. Mad? she thought. Why mad when we needed the money so desperately? . . . Then she continued with her story:

"Then my mother asked, quite coolly, 'Where did he shoot himself?' And Armin answered, just as coolly, 'Behind his right ear.' Mother gave a kind of appreciative nod and said, 'He did well.' But then all her self-control was gone. I'd never seen Mother cry, not even when we lost all our money. She just used to complain. But now she laid her head on the table, her shoulders twitching. 'But, Mother,' Armin said, 'it's better like this.' At that Mother got angry, jumped up and paced round and round the room. All she kept on saying was, 'Twenty-two years! Twenty-two years' "

They could feel that Sonja was going through the scene again, was seeing everything in her mind's eye. Her eyelids were closed. What long lashes the girl had . . .

Studer was daydreaming. So the scene he'd visualized the time he went to see Frau Witschi had been wrong. He'd seen the table, the people sitting round it, Anastasia Witschi telling her husband not to be a coward . . . Yes, it had been like that, surely. But he had seen one person too many at the table: Sonja. Sonja knew nothing about it, had been told nothing until she was presented with a *fait accompli.* And even then she might have refused to play her part if . . . if it hadn't been for those romantic novels. What was one called? *Wrongly Accused.* People like the examining magistrate had no time for that kind of complication. Complication? It was simple . . . Simplicity itself.

But it seemed that a simple detective understood such complications better than a man with a university degree . . . Sonja had come over to the other side . . . Strange, it had all started when the sergeant had dried the girl's tears . . . Things like that were as delicate as the gossamer threads floating in the air in the late summer. You could think about them, but could you talk about them? If you did start talking about that kind of thing, you were sure to get Dr Locard quoted at you. And quite rightly so, quite rightly so!

Funny how voices could change. When she went on, Sonja's voice was deeper and slightly husky:

"Then my brother said to me, 'You're on good terms with Schlumpf — so good you even want to get married. You're to tell him tomorrow that he has to start behaving suspiciously. It's got to look as though he committed the murder. Until the insurance has paid out. Then we'll see that we get him released, no problem.' I refused at first, but not for long. I was so stupid. I've been reading too many novels. In those novels you keep getting a man who sacrifices himself for a woman, lets himself be put in prison rather than betray her. So we discussed the details. I was to go and see Erwin the next evening and give him the three hundred francs, then he was to go the Bear, drink something and pay with a hundred-franc note. My brother rang Corporal Murmann . . ."

The telephone call Murmann had mentioned. The unknown male voice. It *was* all like the plot of a novel! He'd have to have a talk with Armin . . . And what part had the barber's assistant played in the whole affair? Gerber had a motorbike. Did he know how to drive a car as well? He must do. Then Studer needed to know what Cottereau, Ellenberger's head gardener, had seen to make a few lads beat him up so badly. Studer became more and more immersed in his musing. Ellenberger had bought a gun . . . Perhaps two shots after all? Had someone helped Witschi commit suicide? Held his arm, for example? . . . Or had he missed and someone else had . . .

Studer broke the silence that had descended. "Tell me, why did you give Gerber the fountain pen?" As he spoke he could see Gerber in his mind's eye, with his too-red lips and his overall with the blue lapels.

"He saw the two of us together that night, Erwin and me," Sonja said softly. "And he threatened to tell the authorities Erwin was innocent . . ."

"When did he see you?" Studer's question came out sharply.

"The evening it all happened, on the Tuesday, at ten, on the other side of the village, nowhere near the place my father was found."

"Aha," said Studer. Then he concentrated on his typewriting again. The magistrate dictated slowly. He had no difficulty keeping up.

But it was a tedious task nonetheless. The examining magistrate started asking questions, firing them off, probing and probing, he wanted to know everything. It went on for half an hour, for an hour. Even Studer was sweating and Sonja was close to collapse. Only Schlumpf was as upright as ever. He stood by the wall, gave short, clear answers when a question was directed at him. For all that, he did not seem particularly pleased that he would soon be a free man again. Studer could understand him well. The heroic role was over and Schlumpf had not behaved like a hero at all. He had insisted on his innocence, had tried to kill himself . . . No, he had certainly not cut a glorious figure . . . Thank God, Studer thought. He wasn't that keen on heroes. His own private opinion was that it was their weaknesses that endeared people to you . . .

At long, long last the magistrate finished. The barrage of questions had brought out nothing of importance. If Sonja's story could have been recorded on disc, Studer thought, the effect would have been livelier and more accurate than the dry indirect speech of the official written statement. Ah well . . .

"I will of course," the examining magistrate said, after he had graciously allowed Sonja and Schlumpf to retire ("You wait for me, lassie," Studer had told her, "I'll take you home.") "discuss the matter with the state prosecutor, then there will be no obstacle to Schlumpf's release . . ."

"That is just what you mustn't do, sir," said Studer, wagging an admonitory finger and with a strange glint in his eye. "Leave the state prosecutor out of it for the moment. You need confirmation, you need to interrogate the mother and brother before taking any further steps. You must summon Ellenberger for interview. You need confirmation."

"But for God's sake, Studer, it's obvious it's suicide."

Studer was silent. Then he said, "I would like to speak to the car thief."

"Is that necessary?"

"Yes," said Studer.

The magistrate shrugged his shoulders, as if to suggest that this was the kind of thing examining magistrates had to put up with. But he still wanted to put Studer in his place, so he said pointedly, "You quoted Dr Locard just now, didn't you. But . . . you . . ." Faced with Studer's steady gaze he found he couldn't go on. But the pitiless sergeant insisted on

dragging the thought that was in his mind out into
the light of day.

"You're wondering whether I'm not half mad myself?
But my dear sir" — the address made the magistrate
start. The familiarity! — "we're all a bit round the bend.
Some farther than others, of course . . ."

The examining magistrate wasted no time ringing
the bell.

The car thief

He looked like a cross between a dachshund and a greyhound. He had a dachshund's bow legs and a greyhound's pointed head. His name was Hans Augsburger, five previous convictions. He was in danger of getting locked away for a longish stretch.

Studer knew him, although Augsburger generally pursued his profession in other cantons. He was a burglar, but an amateurish bungler, dogged by misfortune. Several times Studer had had to pick him up at the request of other police forces.

"*Salut*, Augsburger," Studer said. He got up from his seat at the typewriter, went over to meet him and shook him by the hand. The policeman at the door gave a look of astonishment at this hearty greeting, but Augsburger was not in the least disconcerted.

"Hey, it's Studer!" he said. "Good to see you, Sergeant."

Then, turning to the examining magistrate: "The sergeant has an open mind, he'll listen to what a man has to say. Got a cigarette for me, Sergeant?"

"Yes — if you don't give us any of your lies." Studer signalled the magistrate to allow him to conduct the interrogation. The magistrate nodded, looked on his desk for the file with Augsburger, Hans: CAR THEFT on the cover and handed it to Studer.

Studer leafed through it. Nothing interesting. "In the course of a regular patrol . . . outside the railway station . . . stopped the driver . . . no licence . . . car on the stolen list . . . did not resist arrest . . ."

"Isn't the list of the things in his possession at the time of arrest in the file?" Studer asked.

"I'm sure it is," said the magistrate. He was playing with his paper-knife again.

"Oh yes, here it is." Studer read out loud:

"1 purse, contents 12.50 francs, 1 handkerchief, 1 shirt, 1 pair of trousers"

And then: "1 Browning pistol, 6.5 calibre."

What?

"Hey, Augsburger, this looks bad. Carrying a gun? Since when have you had a gun? Are you looking for a life sentence, eh?"

Augsburger said nothing.

"I'd like to see the gun," Studer said.

The policeman brought it. "It's loaded," he said.

Studer took the gun and unloaded it. There were six cartridges in the magazine, one in the barrel.

"Did you shoot one, Augsburger?"

Augsburger maintained his silence. But the skin on the right-hand side of his face twitched, like a horse's tormented by flies.

"The barrel's not even been cleaned." Studer was speaking more and more slowly. The magistrate pricked up his ears.

"Six point five," said Studer with a nod. "The same calibre as the bullet in Witschi's head . . ."

"But, Sergeant, we know now that . . ."

"We know nothing, sir, nothing at all. We've been told about a plan to get money as quickly as possible, but the plan has obviously not worked out quite the way it was intended." Seeing Augsburger turn one of his large ears towards him, Studer spoke in as deep and low a voice as possible.

"I keep thinking of what the doctor at the Institute for Forensic Medicine demonstrated to me: the posture

Witschi would have had to adopt to shoot himself just behind his right ear . . . and the lack of powder marks. Admittedly that might be possible with cigarette papers, but I'm not quite convinced. There's more to this case than meets the eye."

Studer stopped abruptly. Augsburger had lowered his eyes.

"Where have you been for the last two weeks?" he suddenly asked.

"In . . . in . . ."

"Here, have a cigarette," said Studer in a friendly voice. It took a while to get it lit.

"Look, Augsburger," said Studer gently, "if you can't prove where you were during the night on which a certain Wendelin Witschi was murdered, then there's only one thing I can say: I . . . But no, in that case I want nothing more to do with you. The jury will know what it has to do in a case of murder in the course of robbery . . ."

"But Schlumpf's confessed to it!" Augsburger exclaimed.

"And has just withdrawn his confession. Or, rather, I proved to him that it was impossible for him to have committed the murder. And then a witness has come forward who is prepared to swear Schlumpf was with them at the supposed time of the murder."

"Then he lied to me," said Augsburger angrily.

"Who?"

"Old Ellenberger."

"Aha. And why did you steal the mayor's car on Saturday night?"

"It was too hot in Gerzenstein," said Augsburger, but his unconcern sounded a little forced.

"And why did you go to the station square in Thun of all places? You must have known a policeman would nab you there?"

"I took a wrong turn. I was meaning to go to Inter-laken . . ."

"So you drove through the town, when every school-boy knows the main road goes round?"

"I needed a drink . . ." His answers were more and more hesitant.

"And where did you steal the gun?"

"The gun?" Augsburger was starting to repeat the question. That was a good sign, Studer knew he'd soon have him. "The gun?" Then very quickly:

"It was on Ellenberger's desk, that's where I took it from."

"Hmm." Studer said nothing. It could be true. Ellenberger had bought a 6.5 Browning in Bern a fort-night ago. Armin had got someone to hide the other gun in Frau Hofmann's kitchen. Who? For the moment it didn't matter.

"You were staying at Ellenberger's?" Studer asked.

"Yes." Augsburger nodded several times.

"In which room?"

"In the attic."

"Why did Ellenberger take you in?"

"Oh, no special reason. Out of pity."

"Did you see the others?"

"Not often. Ellenberger brought my food up to me."

"And he told you to steal the mayor's car, get caught in Thun, then try to persuade Schlumpf to confess?"

"What? What?" The man sounded genuinely sur-prised, but the more it went on, the more it seemed to Studer the man was acting a part.

"Yes, you told Schlumpf to ask to see the examining magistrate and tell him he'd killed Witschi. You must have given him a very compelling reason to make the confession. For example that the idea of a murder wasn't working and people were beginning to think it was suicide and the whole family was in danger of being arrested on suspicion of insurance fraud. And so it was best Schlumpf took everything upon himself. Was that it? If it's true you might as well admit it. We only have to ask Schlumpf."

"We should have done that before," the examining magistrate sighed. "But you go at everything like a bull at a gate, my dear Studer, I can't get a word in . . ."

"You didn't think of it either," Studer replied curtly. "But we can always have Schlumpf brought back. A confrontation . . ."

Studer looked Augsburger straight in the eye. He was clearly growing uneasy.

"But before we go ahead with the confrontation, I have a few more questions for this man."

He was silent for a time while he thought.

"We found the gun on you, Augsburger, you'll never be able to prove you took it off Ellenberger's desk. You see that, don't you? Ellenberger will deny it. You won't be able to prove you were in bed on the Tuesday night in question. Or will Ellenberger be able to confirm that?"

"I . . . I imagine so."

"Good. But who gave you the message for Schlumpf. Come on, tell us."

"It . . . it was Armin Witschi."

"And you were to tell Schlumpf the message came from his sister?"

"Yes."

"Were you alone with him when you spoke? With Armin Witschi, I mean?"

"Yes. There was no one else there."

"How did you know who he was?"

"Oh, you know . . . I'd seen him . . . around . . ."

"I would like to have had a look at the stolen car, but perhaps the mayor has collected it already?"

The examining magistrate nodded. "Yes, yesterday."

"All the better," said Studer. "As soon as I've got anything new, I'll let you know. And you can put Schlumpf back in a single cell. He won't try to hang himself again . . . Cheerio one and all."

Studer particularly liked the "one and all".

He was still laughing to himself as he went down the corridor to collect Sonja.

Visits

Sonja's hands were on Studer's shoulders. He found the light pressure pleasant. It had stopped raining as well, the sky was white. There was a cold wind, but it was behind them so they didn't really feel it. Not a bad machine Murmann had bought himself, either. Didn't make much noise. When Studer looked down at the black tarmac of the road, it had a pattern of white stripes. Everything was fine, except that the sergeant felt somewhat under the weather. His head was aching and on the right side of his chest, fairly low down, he could feel a stabbing pain. At the first inn they came to Studer stopped and ordered a hot toddy. It was his universal remedy.

"Where does the waitress come from, by the way?" he asked. The words seemed to have to drag themselves out of his mouth.

"Which waitress?" Sonja asked.

"At the Bear. Your brother's girlfriend."

"From Zägerschwil. Why, Sergeant?"

"Zägerschwil? Is it far?"

It wasn't that far, Sonja said, only the roads were poor. It was a hamlet, of sorts, in the Emmental. On a hill, the back of beyond . . .

"How do you know?"

"My brother told me. He went up there with her on one of her days off."

"Does Armin mean to marry the girl? She's quite a bit older than he is, isn't she?"

"Yes, she is, but her parents have money, and Berti's got some saved up too. Armin's been to visit her parents a few times."

"Should we go and visit her parents?" Studer asked, ordering a coffee-and-kirsch. He needed to fortify himself. The stabbing pain was slowly disappearing and his headache had lifted, floating away like a light hat carried off on the breeze.

"What would you do there?" Sonja asked.

"Go and see Armin, you idiot. There's a few things I need to ask him."

"You think he's . . ."

"Where else would he be? He hasn't got a passport, so he won't have gone abroad, and he's afraid of the city, isn't he?"

Sonja nodded.

"That only leaves his future parents-in-law then. What are they called?"

Their name was Kräienbühl. And why not? Berta Witschi-Kräienbühl, it sounded good, sounded solid, respectable. Unlike Witschi-Mischler. Names probably accounted for a lot . . . Studer pulled himself together. What crazy ideas he was thinking up. Surreptitiously he placed the fingers of his left hand on his right pulse. A slight fever, certainly, but he couldn't take himself off to bed now. First of all he had to clear up the death of Wendelin Witschi. There was no getting out of that . . . Witschi-Kräienbühl or Kräienbühl-Witschi? Didn't make any difference. Time to go. But the coffee was good, what about another? OK. So Studer drank a second coffee. Sonja dipped a roll in her glass. She was eating. Of course, she'd be hungry, a young thing like that.

Should he take her home first? But she wouldn't get a hot meal for lunch at home.

"Are you hungry, Sonja?" Studer asked. "If you want something to eat, you've only to say. A ham roll?"

Sonja shook her head. "Later," she said.

Kräienbühl-Mischler, Aeschbacher-Ellenberger, Gerber-Murmann ... Just a minute. What was the maiden name of the corporal's wife? Studer tried out so many combinations his head was starting to spin. He stood up.

"All right then, off we go." He had difficulty picking up the change from the table, but he managed, with Sonja's help.

And he continued to manage when he was back in the saddle of Murmann's bike. Sonja gave him directions. There were some terrible roads, with deep ruts. The machine reared and bucked as if they were in a motor-bike scramble. Studer felt he was riding in a dream.

At last, one final uphill (Studer had had to ask the way from Bangerten) and they were there. A large farm, an old gateway. All was quiet, there was no one to be seen. Studer crossed the farmyard. The door to the kitchen was ajar, he knocked.

"Yes!" an impatient voice shouted.

"Hi there, Armin," said Studer in friendly tones. "Sonja's come too."

He looked a bit dishevelled, did Armin Witschi. His hair did not rise up over his low forehead in such tri-umphant waves as before.

"Sergeant!" he stammered.

"Shhh," said Studer, placing a finger to his lips. "Not everyone needs to know the police are looking for you. It's just a friendly visit, see, you can stay up here till everything's quietened down. Can anyone hear us?" he suddenly asked.

Armin shook his head. Now, on his own, he didn't seem so arrogant. There was no mocking smile on his lips, he was an ordinary, frightened lad whose only desire seemed to be to get out of an unpleasant business as quickly as possible.

"Why did you run off? I knew right away you would, you know, yesterday afternoon when Berta gave you the sign from the doorway. But what did you need five hundred francs for? There's nothing to spend it on up here."

He hadn't intended to stay here, Armin said. He'd been going to slip across the border, make his way to Paris. He had a friend there, he'd be able to fix him up with a passport.

Where were the Kräienbühls?

Planting out their beans, Armin thought.

Good, said Studer. What he needed to know could be put in a few words. The sergeant took his notebook out of his pocket. As he did so he could feel his heart pounding hard and fast — but it wasn't the Witschi case that was giving the sergeant palpitations.

"Your sister's told us everything. We'll have to see if we can sort out this matter of insurance fraud, 'cause that's what we're talking about presumably, if . . . If — there's the rub. But you must give me some clear answers. What was the agreement you made with your father?"

And Armin Witschi did give a clear answer. He was very subdued, too subdued almost. That was the problem with that kind of character, Studer thought. They're all swagger when they've got an audience but get them by themselves and they have their tails between their legs in no time at all.

For a long time his father had refused to fake an accident, but eventually, when Ellenberger wouldn't give them any more money and they were up to their necks in debt, he had agreed.

The plan was that he was to shoot himself in the leg,

wait until Armin had removed the gun, then shout. Someone was sure to come, Ellenberger's tree nursery was quite close to the spot they'd chosen. Witschi would claim he'd been held up and robbed.

"We thought it would be best to do the business (the business, Armin said!) late one evening. Then when father told his story people would believe him when he said he hadn't recognized his attacker. It would save him from being pestered with lengthy questioning and suspicion would fall on Ellenberger's employees, since they've all got records. But they'd be able to prove their innocence and none of them would go down for it. The case would be closed and the insurance would pay out . . ."

"Hmm," Studer growled. "But things didn't work out like that, did they?"

"We agreed on an evening when father would be coming home with some money. We even talked about it, that is father mentioned it to Ellenberger when his workers were there. We'd arranged that. Father had a Browning pistol."

"Who gave it him?"

"Ellenberger bought it in Bern."

"Are you sure of that?"

"Yes. Ellenberger knew about the whole business. As did Uncle Aeschbacher."

"Oh he did, did he?"

"Mother told him. He is a relation, after all."

"And the mayor . . ." Studer said softly, rocking his head from side to side, like an old Jew who's just seen the meaning of an obscure passage of the Talmud.

"Yes. Father tried out the gun, sticking cigarette papers in the barrel until he knew how to do it without leaving any powder marks. Then on the evening in question I waited for him. Starting at ten. I heard his

166

Zehnder, he got off, as we'd agreed, he saw me, even gave me a wave, put his wallet, his watch, his pen —"

"Parker Duofold," said Studer in the voice of a salesman praising his wares.

"That's right. He put them down beside the motor-bike and went into the woods. It was a long time before I heard the shot. And not just one shot, but two. That surprised me, because the second shot came right after the first. I couldn't work out what was going on. If he hadn't wounded himself with the first, it would be stupid to fire another without stuffing some cigarette papers down the barrel beforehand, and that took time . . ."

Silence. Sonja gave a brief sigh, took out her crumpled handkerchief and wiped her eyes. Studer put his hand over hers.

"Don't cry, lassie," he said. "It's like at the dentist's. It's only when he puts the forceps on the tooth that it hurts, after that it's all over in a flash." Sonja managed a faint smile.

The wood crackled in the kitchen stove; drops of water splashed from a pan lid onto the hot plate and hissed. The wax-cloth cover of the table at which the three of them were sitting felt greasy and cold. Through the open door a lonely hen could be seen vainly trying to scratch up the cobbles. It was very busy, the little white hen, and very quiet . . .

"I went into the woods. I was looking for father. We'd agreed on a spot so I wouldn't have to spend long looking for the gun. It took some time before I found him, he was in a quite different place."

"In a different place? Are you sure of that?"

"Yes. We'd agreed to meet at a big beech, but he was lying a good thirty yards away, under a pine tree."

"That's right, underneath a pine tree. Fortunately . . ." Studer said softly.

"Why fortunately?" Sonja asked her voice choked with sobs.

"Because otherwise I wouldn't have noticed there were no pine needles on the back of your father's coat."

The two gave each other an astonished look, but Studer waved their questions away. The stabbing pain was back, his head felt hot. The last thing he wanted was to have to explain things!

"He was lying under a pine tree with a bullet hole behind his right ear. I'd taken a torch, so I could see it. The gun was beside his hand."

"Right or left?"

"Just a minute, Sergeant, I have to think about that. His arms were stretched out, either side of his head, and the gun was between them."

"That's not much help," said Studer.

"I picked up the gun and went home. On the way I tried to think what we should do. Father was dead. Perhaps that was best for him. I knew Uncle Aeschbacher was just looking for an opportunity to get him committed to hard labour in Witzwil or St Johannsen."

"Did you collect the wallet and the other things immediately after your father put them down?"

"No, not straight away. Something happened. I heard a car approaching . . ."

"Where was it coming from? From the village or the other direction?"

"From the village, I think."

"I think! I think! Can't you be certain?"

"No. When I heard it I went farther into the woods."

"On the side of the road where your father was or on the other side?"

"On the other side. Afterwards I had to cross the road."

168

"And there wasn't a car there any longer?"

"No. But there was something odd about the car. It was going very slowly, I could tell by the sound of the engine, and the headlights lit up the road, and the woods too, even though they were a long way off. I threw myself to the ground so as not to be seen. There's a curve above and below that stretch, so it's difficult to tell which direction a car's coming from," Armin added apologetically.

"And?"

"Oh yes. Suddenly the lights went out and I couldn't hear the engine any more. I waited for some time, then I crawled slowly closer to the road. But the car had gone."

Ellenberger had a small lorry to transport his trees. Ellenberger had paid the life insurance premiums . . .

"Then you picked up the things your father had left at the edge of the woods and went home?"

"Yes." Armin nodded.

"D'you want to come to Bern with me, Sonja?" Studer asked. "I think we've learnt all we need to here." Studer took out his watch. "We should be there about two. We could go to our flat and get something to eat, then you could wait for me there. I'll take you home this evening. By the way, who hid the gun at Frau Hofmann's? Gerber? I thought so."

The use of a microscope

It was around ten o'clock in the evening when the night bell rang at Dr Neuenschwander's (surgery 8–9 am). The doctor was a tall, bony man in his late thirties with a long face, well-known and well-liked throughout the district. He had the strange habit of sending the rich farmers very large bills. On the other hand, when visiting other people he would sometimes forget a twenty-franc note or a five-franc piece on the kitchen table. He could get very angry if it was pointed out to him.

When he heard the bell, he was sitting at his desk in his shirt-sleeves. He went through a mental list of patients who might need him, but couldn't remember any serious cases.

"An accident, perhaps," he muttered and went to the door.

Outside was a sturdy man in a blue raincoat. The doctor couldn't quite see his face under the broad brim of his black felt hat.

"What's up?" he asked irritably.

Did the doctor have a microscope?

A what?

A microscope.

Yes, of course he had one. But what for? And at this time of night? Couldn't it wait till morning?

No.

The man in the blue raincoat shook his head vigorously. Then he introduced himself: Sergeant Studer of the cantonal Criminal Investigation Department.

"Come in," said the doctor in broad Swiss, shaking his head as he led his late visitor into his surgery. "Witschi case?" he asked laconically.

Studer nodded.

The doctor took the light-coloured case out of the cupboard where he kept his microscope, placed it on the table, went to the tap, washed a glass slide, dipped it in alcohol, dried it.

Studer pulled an envelope out of his pocket. Carefully he shook out a tiny amount of the contents onto the slide, put a drop of water on it and placed a second, even thinner slide on top.

"Stain?" the doctor asked.

"Not necessary." Studer's face was bright red, from time to time his throat gave out an unpleasant croaking noise, his eyes were bloodshot. The doctor had a look at the sergeant, went up to him, put on his horn-rimmed spectacles, had a closer look, then silently took his wrist and said dryly, "When you're done I'll examine you. I don't like the look of you, Sergeant, not one little bit."

Studer's response was the hoarse rasp of a painful cough.

"You're messing around with pleurisy there. Get to your bed, man, get to your bed."

"Tomorrow," Studer said with a groan, "tomorrow afternoon, if you insist, Doctor. But I've so much still to do . . . though the most important things are sorted out, and if this here . . ."

Studer arranged the microscope so that the bright light from the desk lamp fell on the little mirror, and bent down over the eyepiece. He adjusted the focus, but his fingers were trembling so much he couldn't get the right setting. At one point he kept twisting and turning the knob so much, the doctor stopped him.

"You'll break the slide," he exclaimed in irritation.

"You focus it, Doctor," Studer said meekly. "My damn fingers won't stop trembling."

"What is it you're looking for that's so important?"

"Traces of powder," Studer croaked.

"Aha!" said Dr Neuenschwander and began to turn the knob little by little.

"Clearly visible," he said at last, straightening up. "I'm not a forensic scientist, but I can remember from my student days. Look, Sergeant, there: the big circles are drops of fat and in them you can see the yellow crystals. Picric acid. That's it for sure, though whether it would be accepted in court as proof, I don't know."

"That will probably not be necessary," said Studer, speaking with difficulty. "And forgive me for disturbing you at such a late hour, Doctor."

"Don't be silly," said Neuenschwander. "But you must tell me" — his index finger pointed at the envelope — "where you got that dust. Stop. Not now. First of all take off your jacket and shirt, then lie down on that couch so I can have a listen and see what's going on inside your chest. Then I'll give you something to help you through the night."

Dr Neuenschwander listened through his stethoscope and tapped Studer's chest, tapped and listened. He seemed particularly interested in the spot where Studer could feel the stabbing pain. He stuck a thermometer under his armpit, shook his head when he looked at the reading and said, the concern audible in his voice, "A hundred and two." He took his pulse again, muttered something like, "Of course, Brissagos," then went over to a glass-fronted cupboard. As he filled the little syringe from an ampoule, he said:

"Right, Sergeant, it's straight off to bed for you. I'm giving you some pretty strong stuff here. If you have a good sweat during the night, you can finish off what you have to do tomorrow. But at your own risk, understood? And when you've finished with all your rushing around, you'll be ripe for a hospital bed. If I were you I'd book a taxi and go straight there. You can count yourself lucky it's a dry pleurisy. But it can get worse. And now I really would like to know why you've come looking for a microscope so late at night. But hold on a minute." He poured various liquids from different bottles into a glass, added some water and gave it to Studer to drink. It tasted horrible. Studer shook himself. Then he got an injection as well and could put his clothes back on. He started to stand up.

"Stay lying down," the doctor barked.

And Studer stayed lying down. The lamp on the desk had a green metal shade, the shelves along the wall were filled with large tomes. The room had a dispensary smell. Studer lay on his back, hands clasped behind his neck.

"So?" the doctor asked.

Studer took a deep breath. It was the first time that day he'd been able to breathe in deeply.

"The traces of gunpowder," he said, "were the last link in the chain of proof — as they say in those novels. I didn't really need it, everything was clear already . . ."

And he told the doctor about his journey to Thun, Sonja's statement, their visit to Armin Witschi, the drive to Bern.

"I've used a microscope once already today," he said, smiling up at the ceiling. Large beads of sweat were running down his face, now and then he wiped his hand across his forehead. "And do you know, Doctor," suddenly Studer was speaking formal German, though this time it wasn't his anger that made him forget his native dialect, but the fever, "the bullet that was found in the head of Herr Wendelin Witschi — the Wendelin Witschi who, according to Dr Giuseppe Malapelle of the Institute for Forensic Medicine in Bern, was an alcoholic corpse with a blood-alcohol level of over two hundred — the bullet came from the gun I found on that bungling burglar, Hans Augsburger, this morning."

Studer giggled like a little schoolboy. "If the examining magistrate knew I'd pinched the gun! A good lad, the examining magistrate, but young. And we're so old. Aren't we, Doctor? Ancient. We understand everything, we have to understand everything . . . What was it Frau Hofmann said? 'Judge not, that ye be not judged.' Quite right, too. Excellent. Who else said that? I can't remember . . . Anyway, after that it was easy to solve the question of where the gun came from . . . But Studer's not telling. — It's so hot in here, Doctor. Have you got a fire in May too, like the examining magistrate? . . . I had a splendid dream once, a dream of a thumbprint, a gigantic thumbprint . . . You don't go in for the interpretation of thumbs, er . . . the interpretation of dreams, do you, Doctor? I had a case to investigate in a lunatic asylum once. I had to deal with a man who was a . . . just a minute, what's it called? Oh yes, he was a psychoanalyst. He could interpret dreams and he'd tell you exactly what was the matter with you. He died, the psychoanalyst did, despite all his interpreting of dreams . . . But what was I going to tell you? . . . Everything's getting all mixed up . . . You wanted to know where I found the traces of gunpowder? . . . Just a moment . . . You know Cottereau? The head gardener? Yes? What do you think of him? Getting a bit old, second childhood? Am I right? He knew something, but a few lads beat him up. He saw him, you know, the one who . . . I'm not naming names. Cottereau saw him that evening — or that night, if you prefer . . . When does it stop being evening and start being night? Could you give me a definition, doctor? . . . You know the pockets they have down the side of car doors. Where people usually keep their maps? That dust in the envelope, I scraped it out of one of those pockets. . . . The last link, doctor. Sergeant Studer's not going to end up with egg on his face . . . But Sergeant Studer has no idea how the the affair's going to end . . . No idea. Just imagine . . . I need to sleep," Studer said suddenly. He closed his mouth, his wrinkled lids came down over his eyes, he gave a deep sigh . . .

"Poor fellow," Dr Neuenschwander said. He went out to fetch a neighbour and the two of them carried Studer up to the guest room, undressed him and tucked him up warmly in bed. Neuenschwander filled a hot-water bottle as well and put it by Studer's feet, which were ice-cold. He left the door to the bedroom open and went back to his desk. There he read until one o'clock, going to check on the sergeant every hour. He must have been having troubled dreams. He kept murmuring, almost always the same words. The doctor could make out "microscope" and "thumb-print". And a girl's name: "Sonja."

At four Dr Neuenschwander got up again. Studer's temperature had gone down to ninety-eight point six.

A hot toddy with the mayor

A dreary funeral. Naturally it had started raining again. Scarcely had you pulled your shoe out of the clinging, clayey soil of the graveyard than the footprint filled with yellow water. There were only ten umbrellas gathered round Wendelin Witschi's grave and the raindrops falling on the ten opened umbrellas beat out a soft, sad drum-roll.

The pastor was brief. Sonja sobbed. Frau Witschi stood next to her, ramrod straight. She wasn't crying. Armin had not come. After the pastor, Aeschbacher said a few words. They cost him a visible effort.

Studer was next to Dr Neuenschwander and was glad to have the doctor's arm to lean on. But as they were slowly making their way to the graveyard gate, the sergeant let go of his arm, caught up with the mayor and said, "I need to talk to you, Mayor."

"To me, Sergeant?"

"Yes," Studer said.

"Come along, then."

Aeschbacher's car was parked in the street. The mayor opened the door, wedged himself into the seat behind the steering wheel and waved Studer over. The sergeant got in, shook the doctor's hand in farewell, then closed the door on his side.

Neither of the men was what you could call slim and there wasn't a lot of room. Aeschbacher pressed the starter. Studer stared at the pocket in the side of the door.

Aeschbacher said nothing. He turned the car and drove back into the village, past all the shop signs. Gerzenstein, village of shops and wireless sets. When had Studer called the village that? A long time ago? On Saturday. And today was Tuesday. Only two days between then and now!

The wireless sets were silent. Either it was too early, or the noise of the car was drowning out the music and speech.

The village of Gerzenstein. A village? Where were the farmers in the village? They were nowhere in evidence. Presumably they lived somewhere in the background, behind the façade of shops.

Aeschbacher wheezed. There must be a lot weighing heavily on the man's mind.

And as the car turned into Bahnhofstrasse, on the short drive from the main road to the *Gerzenstein Advertiser* printing works, Studer went through the previous evening in his mind once more:

Cottereau who had finally decided to speak. Cottereau who had seen the mayor put the gun in one of those pockets they have in the side of car doors. Cottereau who remembered it well. He'd gone for a walk that evening, that Tuesday evening. And he'd seen every one of the characters in the little drama. He'd seen Schwomm, out for a walk with a girl from the third year of the secondary school (which explained the teacher's suspicious silence), and Wendelin Witschi, who had dismounted from his Zehnder and disappeared into the woods; he'd recognized Aeschbacher's car, seen the mayor follow Witschi . . .

"I think we'd better go into the house," said Aeschbacher. The car had stopped outside a wrought-iron gate with gilded spikes. There was the arc lamp with the stiff, red tulips round its base, there was the station with the kiosk where Anastasia Witschi read novels while she was waiting for her customers. Anastasia Witschi who was related to the mayor . . .

What was it she'd said when she heard her husband was dead? "Twenty-two years." And had paced round and round the room.

"As you like," Studer replied to Aeschbacher's question, which wasn't a question at all but an invitation. He observed the fat man unobtrusively out of the corner of his eye.

Offices. Girls sitting at typewriters suddenly began to hammer away at the keys when Aeschbacher appeared in the doorway.

"Good morning, sir, good morning, Mayor."

An old man, almost a dwarf, intercepted Aeschbacher. He was holding a printed sheet. His index finger, which he was running along the lines of print, was deformed at the end. Studer saw it all with crystal clarity. At the same time he was in a wretched state. His legs felt as if they were made from old bits of flannel, stitched together and filled with wood shavings.

Aeschbacher seemed too preoccupied to respond to the white dwarf's long-winded explanations with more than a few vague words. He was in a hurry to get on. He took off his hat. The lock of brown hair still stuck to his forehead.

A small door . . . the staircase . . . on the first floor the door to his apartment. Beside the door, a brass plate with "Aeschbacher" in black letters on it. No Christian name, no "mayor", nothing. It fitted the man.

"Come in, Sergeant," Aeschbacher said. Was the mayor's voice cracking slightly? It still sounded like the voice of the announcer on Radio Bern, but something about it had changed. Or, Studer wondered, has my hearing sharpened? The fever?

178

He was in the corridor of the apartment. The kitchen door was open. There was a smell of sauerkraut and bacon fat. Studer felt sick. He hadn't touched a thing since yesterday's lunch. His stomach had gone on strike. How long was he going to have to stand in this corridor?

A woman came out of the kitchen. She was small and thin and her hair was as white as lilac. Yes, white as lilac. She had grey eyes with a very quiet look. It couldn't always be that easy, being the wife of Mayor Aeschbacher.

"My wife," said Aeschbacher. And, "Sergeant Studer."

A look of mild surprise in the grey eyes, quickly replaced by anxiety. "Nothing bad has happened, I hope?" she asked in a quiet voice.

"No, no," said Aeschbacher reassuringly, placing his huge, fat hand on his wife's slim shoulder, a gesture so tender Studer suddenly felt he knew the mayor much better than before. Things in life were always different from the way you imagined. A man might be brutal, but not all the time, at others, apparently, he could be quite different . . .

A large room, probably intended as a smoking room. A few pictures on the walls. Studer knew nothing about painting, but he liked them. Large reproductions, colourful, sunflowers, a landscape in the south of France, a few engravings. The wallpaper was grey, the carpet white with a black-and-red pattern.

"My wife furnished the room," said Aeschbacher. "Sit down, Sergeant. What will you drink?"

"Whatever you like," Studer replied, "as long as it's not raspberry cordial or beer."

"Brandy? Yes? You don't look well, Sergeant. What's wrong? Shall I get my wife to make you a hot toddy. You're partial to a hot toddy, I believe?"

An awkward situation. Why was this Aeschbacher being so polite? What was behind it?

The mayor went out, after offering Studer a cigar. It was a good cigar, not a cheap cigar, but it still tasted like burnt rubber. Studer forced himself to take a pull on it.

Aeschbacher returned. He was carrying three bottles: brandy, gin, whisky. Behind him came his wife. She put a tray down on the table: sugar, slices of lemon, a jug of hot water, two glasses.

"We must look after our sergeant," said Aeschbacher with a smile that sent his tom-cat moustache sticking out in all directions, "he's caught a cold. And a detective with a cold might find it difficult to carry out an arrest, might he not, Sergeant?"

And Aeschbacher patted Studer on the knee. Studer was going to ask him to refrain from such familiarity and looked up — to meet a look from the mayor, a pleading look.

Studer understood. The mayor knew. He was asking for his wife to be spared. "Fine by me," thought Studer. He laughed.

"Goodbye then, sergeant," said Frau Aeschbacher. She had her hand on the door-knob and was smiling. A smile that cost her a great effort. Studer suddenly realized that both of them were putting on an act. They were both aware what was happening, but neither wanted to let the other one know.

A strange marriage, Mayor Aeschbacher's marriage . . .

The door was closed gently. The two men were left alone.

Aeschbacher put sugar in one of the glasses, filled it half full with hot water, stirred it, then added a decent helping from each of the three bottles:

brandy, gin, whisky. Studer watched him, eyes wide.

When Aeschbacher offered him the glass he asked, in slightly worried tones, "Is that for me?"

"It's excellent, Sergeant," said the mayor, praising his own concoction. "I drink nothing else when I have a cold. And if it's a bit too much for you, my wife can always make you a coffee later on."

"On your own head be it, then," said Studer and emptied the glass. He had a vague feeling that staying sober wasn't going to be the best way to get this business over with. "But you have to join me."

"Goes without saying," said Aeschbacher, making up another glass of the same mixture.

Studer felt a pleasant warmth creep over his body. Slowly, very slowly the dark curtain rose. Perhaps everything wasn't going to be as awful, as complicated as he had imagined. Aeschbacher sank back into a deep armchair, took a cigar, lit it, emptied his glass, said, "Aah," stayed silent for a moment, then asked in a detached voice, "Did you find what you were looking for in my garage yesterday evening?"

Studer took a puff at his cigar (it suddenly tasted much better) and answered calmly, "Yes."

"What did you find there?"

"Dust."

"That all?"

"It was enough."

A pause. Aeschbacher seemed to be thinking. Then he said, "Dust? In the map pocket?"

"Yes."

"Pity . . . You should have accepted the offer I made you on Sunday. If you want, I could add a bit, out of my own pocket . . . Clever of you to go scratching round in the pocket. No one would have thought of that."

"Your offer?" Studer asked. "What exactly do you mean by that, Aeschbacher?"

The other man gave a start. It was probably being addressed as "Aeschbacher". Not "mayor" any longer, simply "Aeschbacher". Like "Schlumpf".

"I mean the job with my acquaintance, Studer."

"Oh yes, now I remember. I'm not interested, Aeschbacher, not in the least interested. And money? You were offering me money? From what I heard, you're close to bankruptcy."

"Haha," laughed Aeschbacher. It sounded put on. "That's just a story I spread abroad so Witschi would leave me in peace. I had no intention of throwing away all my money to keep him quiet just because I happen to be related to his wife."

"Aha. So you gave Witschi money?"

"Sergeant," said Aeschbacher irritatedly, "we're not playing Jass. Let's put our cards on the table, shall we. If there's something you want to know, then ask, I'll give you your answer. I've been fed up with the whole business for some time now."

"Fine," said Studer, "if that's what you want."

He leant back, crossed his legs and waited.

And during the silence which lay over the room, many things went through his mind. But he couldn't get all the pieces to fall into place. The guilty party had been found. Fine, but where did that get him? The examining magistrate would never agree to interrogate Aeschbacher. No state prosecutor would prefer charges against the mayor. Only if the evidence was so conclusive they had no other choice. Aeschbacher must have been a man to be reckoned with in his day. That had become clear from all the enquiries Studer had made in Bern the previous afternoon. They wanted to avoid a scandal at all costs. And what evidence did Studer have? Cottereau's statement? God, Cottereau would never dare repeat it in court. His examination of the dust under the microscope? It was enough for him. But for a jury, a jury that would be made up of farmers? They'd laugh him out of court. Even the examining magistrate would . . .

Where did that leave him? Let the matter rest there? Witschi had committed suicide? That could be proved, easily proved, the examining magistrate was convinced already. Schlumpf would be released — and the Witschis would have to sell their house, the old woman would carry on reading her novels in the kiosk, Armin would marry the waitress and buy a farm. And Sonja? Sonja would marry Schlumpf, eventually Erwin would be made head gardener. And Aeschbacher? God, he wouldn't be the only murderer running around unpunished . . .

"You're quite right, Sergeant," Aeschbacher's voice echoed through the silence, "there's no point in taking the matter any further. You'll just be left with egg on your face. Didn't it happen once before, in that bank affair? Take your captain's advice. It's better that way, Studer, believe me. Another hot toddy?"

"Please," said Studer, then sank back into silence. Remarkable, wasn't it, that Aeschbacher could read his thoughts? Studer shivered. The stabbing pain in his chest was back. He broke out in a cold sweat. Outside, grey fog had settled at the windows as if the clouds had fallen to earth. And then it was cold in the room. Studer's cigar had gone out and the effort to light it again was too much for him, everything was too much for him just now, he was ill, he should be in bed, he had pleurisy, for God's sake! And with pleurisy you should take yourself off to bed, not play the sharp-witted English detective with deductions à la Sherlock

Holmes. Dust in the map pocket of a car! So what? Next thing he'd be crawling round the floor with a magnifying glass in his hand scouring the carpet for clues!

"Drink up, Studer," said Aeschbacher, pushing the full glass across the table. Obediently Studer emptied it.

He continued to mull things over. It was scandalous really. There you were, with a salary of a few hundred francs a month, you could live on it, sure, live on it reasonably well even. And for those measly few hundred francs a month you were expected to clean out the sewers. Worse than that. You were expected to nose around, uncover other people's misdeeds, get involved here, there and everywhere, without a moment's rest, couldn't even look after yourself properly when you were ill . . .

Aeschbacher took a delighted pull on his cigar. There was a gloating, malicious glint in his little eyes.

And suddenly Studer was back in the dream he'd had. The gigantic thumbprint on the blackboard, Schwomm in his white coat and Aeschbacher with his arm round Sonja, laughing at him, Studer . . .

Afterwards Studer couldn't say whether it was the memory of the dream that had suddenly revitalized him. Or was it the mocking grin on Aeschbacher's face that had got on his nerves? Whatever it was, he pulled himself together, placed his legs apart, rested his forearms on his thighs, clasped his hands and stared at the floor. He spoke slowly, for he had the feeling his tongue might have ideas of going its own way.

"OK," he said, "you're right. I will end up with egg on my face. But that's not the point, Aeschbacher. I do my job, the job I'm paid to do. I'm paid to carry out investigations. I've taken an oath to tell the truth. You'll laugh, I know, Aeschbacher. The truth! But I'm not a babe in arms either. I realize that the truth I find is not the real truth. However, I do know untruth very well. If I give up, and Schlumpf is released, and the case is closed, as they say, then all well and good. After all, I'm not a judge and you're the one who has to live with what you've done." Studer was speaking more and more slowly. He didn't look up, he didn't want to meet Aeschbacher's eyes, he kept staring resolutely at a motif in the carpet pattern, a black square with red threads running through it. God knows why, but it made him think of the back of Witschi's head. Of the thin hair with trickles of blood running down it, to be precise.

"You have to live with it, that's the point. And I don't know if you can. You like a gamble, Aeschbacher, you gamble with people, gamble on the stock exchange, gamble in politics. I've heard a few things about you. I'd be happy to let you go free . . . But then there's the business with Sonja. Sonja, Aeschbacher, Sonja. She's not had much of a life. You sat her on your knee once and her father came in . . . Was Witschi really wrong in his accusation? No, don't say anything. You can have your say when I've finished. I'm no prude. I can understand a bit of fun, Aeschbacher. But there are limits. You've a lot on your conscience, not just Wendelin Witschi. And I don't want you to have Sonja on your conscience as well. Do you follow?"

The clouds outside had sunk even lower, it had become murky in the room. Aeschbacher was enveloped in his chair, Studer could only see his knees. There was a hoarse croaking noise. Was it a throat being cleared or a laugh suppressed.

"I didn't manage to find out what other things Witschi had on you." Speaking was easier now, but Studer still spoke slowly. The strangest thing was that he seemed to have split into two. He could see the room from above, could see himself sitting in his chair, leaning forward, hands clasped, and he thought to himself, "You look like a pastor, Studer, making a visit of condolence." But that passed too, and the examining magistrate's room flashed into his mind, Schlumpf with his head in the girl's lap . . .

"But we can always find out," said Studer, "if necessary. I have heard you've used the money of wards of court for speculation — you're on the Board of Guardians for the area, aren't you? I also heard that you paid the money back, but that Witschi knew about it. He was on the Welfare Commission with you, wasn't he? You don't need to say anything. I'm just telling you all this so you don't think Studer's a fool. Sergeant Studer knows a thing or two . . ."

Silence. Studer got up, still not looking Aeschbacher in the face, grasped one of the bottles, poured himself a drink, knocked back the fiery liquid, sat down again and took a Brissago out of his case. Odd, but it tasted good. His heart still seemed to be jumping all over the place. But, he thought, I'll go to hospital this afternoon. It'll be nice and quiet there.

"Shall I tell you the way it was, Aeschbacher, the whole thing? You don't need to say anything. Not even yes or no. It's more for my own benefit I'm telling the story."

Studer clasped his hands again and stared at the motif in the carpet pattern, the black square with red threads . . .

"Your cousin told you what Witschi was going to do. You found out from her when Witschi intended to carry out his plan. But you didn't trust him. You knew Witschi was a coward — blackmailers are always cowards, for God's sake — and you thought he wouldn't have the guts to injure himself. So you drove to the

186

spot, you knew exactly where it was to happen. Augsburger was staying with you at the time. Why did you
take the man in? Were you jealous of Ellenberger?
Wanted an ex-convict of your own? Well, that's neither
here nor there. So you drove to the place, and you
counted on Armin getting out of the way when he
heard your car coming. Which he did. That gave you
plenty of time to go through Witschi's wallet. I presume the document he was using to blackmail you was
in it? Then you went into the woods. It was easy to
follow Witschi, he made enough noise. Then everything was quiet and you waited. You heard a shot and
went over. Witschi was there, the gun in his hand —
uninjured. What you said to him, I don't know. I'm
sure you played your part well. Arm round his shoulders, probably, comforting him, taking him a bit farther into the woods. You had your own gun in your
pocket. Then you said goodbye, started to walk away
from him, perhaps three feet, then you shot him from
behind."

Pause. Studer took a sip of his drink. Strange, but he
didn't feel at all drunk. On the contrary, he was sober-
ing up, his head seemed to be getting clearer and the
unpleasant stabbing pain had gone. He made a fuss of
relighting his Brissago, which had gone out while he
was talking.

"Two mistakes, Aeschbacher, two big mistakes."
Studer said, like a schoolteacher to a star pupil, not
reprimanding him but helping him to improve.

"First mistake: why didn't you use Witschi's gun?
Armin would have found it, the whole plan would have
gone off like clockwork. At most I would have worked
out that it was suicide, nothing more.

And the second mistake, which led to all the rest:
why leave the gun in the side-pocket of your car?

Someone was bound to find it. That it was that bungling burglar Augsburger of all people was just bad luck. Or was it? Perhaps that was what you intended?"

Studer had finally managed to drag his eyes away from the black-and-red motif. He found himself staring at another that looked like a house and he remembered a little rhyme written in blue on a wall where the paint was beginning to flake off: "Step right in, a welcome guest/ Brings good luck and happiness."

"It's a funny thing about us humans," Studer went on, "sometimes we do the very thing we want to avoid, the very thing our reason warns us not to do. An acquaintance of mine — he's dead now — always used to talk of the subconscious. As if the subconscious had a will of its own. And you remind me of that, Aeschbacher. You've done everything you could to draw attention to yourself. Your passion for gambling might be an explanation, but I think there's something else behind it. I think that deep down inside you wanted the murder to come out. Otherwise you wouldn't have sent Gerber and Armin out in your car to knock Ellenberger and Cottereau down. Who told you Cottereau had seen you? Augsburger?"

"I took Augsburger with me when I went to meet Witschi." The voice from the other side of the room was perfectly calm. Not a quiver of unease. It sounded just like the voice of the announcer when he said, "There has been extensive flooding in the area round the River Rhône . . ."

"And you weren't afraid he'd inform on you?"

"He's a good lad. Later on I'd have sent him abroad."

"But he was wanted. And the car theft . . .?"

"God," said Aeschbacher, "people like that aren't as worried about losing a few years of their lives as we are."

Studer nodded. It was true.

"And I told the other two lads," Aeschbacher went on, "that some plod was sticking his nose in our affairs . . . They've read a lot of detective stories, those two have, they were happy to help. Playing at being John Kling."

For a moment Studer was almost overcome with pride. He had got Aeschbacher to speak, had forced him into a confession. Then he looked up, for the first time, and the feeling of pride melted away. Sitting opposite him, breathing heavily, was a man slumped in a deep armchair. His face was flushed, his mouth slightly open, his hands trembling. But he only stayed like that for a moment. Then the mouth closed and the eyes looked straight ahead once more, past Studer, out of the window.

"Those two lads," said Studer, "gave poor Cottereau a pretty thorough beating-up. He refused to say anything to me. Did Ellenberger know about this business as well?"

"Afterwards, perhaps. At first Cottereau had no idea I'd shot Witschi. It was just a precaution I took to stop him telling you he'd seen me there."

"When did he see you?"

"As I got back into the car. That was when Augsburger saw him. Cottereau, I mean."

If only, Studer thought, I could make a recording of this conversation.

"Why did you get Augsburger to steal your car and take it to Thun and get arrested? That was the idea, wasn't it?"

"Don't ask such stupid questions, Sergeant." It was the mayor speaking. "Of course I got him to do it. Two reasons. One: he might have heard of the reward you were offering, and two: I wanted to put a stop to your little game. If Schlumpf confessed then you'd be stymied, wouldn't you? And Augsburger knew Schlumpf. I told him to try to make contact and tell him from Sonja that things were bad and he had to confess, otherwise they'd all be arrested for insurance fraud. Of course, I didn't expect the people in Thun to be so obliging as to put Augsburger in the same cell as Schlumpf. He wasn't very good at making up a story, I know, he hasn't much imagination. That's why he tried to shift the blame onto Ellenberger."

"Ah yes, Ellenberger," said Studer, in a friendly voice, as if asking a colleague for information. "What do you think of Ellenberger?"

"Huh," said Aeschbacher. "You know the type. Empty inside, so they always have to be busy, always up to something. Their tongues wag, they seek attention, go on about their friend the French Resident in Morocco, about their wealth, set up the Convict Band . . . For me the only positive thing about Ellenberger was that he liked Schlumpf."

Silence. That was it. Now the most difficult part. How should he go about making the arrest? He was pretty shaky, he was ill, and Aeschbacher was a big, heavy man. The telephone he might have used to summon Murmann was in the opposite corner. He did have a gun in his pocket, and a warrant. Still . . .

"You're wondering, Sergeant, how best to go about arresting me? Am I right?" Aeschbacher was saying in his calm voice. "You don't need to worry, I'll come to Thun with you. But we're going in my car, and I'm driving. Is your nerve up to that?"

Aeschbacher had not only guessed Studer's thoughts, he had touched a sensitive spot.

"Afraid? Me?" Studer asked, offended. "Let's go."

"I . . . would just . . . like to . . . say goodbye to my wife." The words came haltingly. Studer nodded.

At the door Aeschbacher said, "Help yourself, sergeant," gesturing towards the bottles on the table.

Studer helped himself. Then he sank back into his chair and closed his eyes. He was tired, dog-tired. The feeling of pride had gone. He had lost the thread. Why had Aeschbacher admitted everything? Had he realized Studer was the only one who knew all about it? Was that why he was suggesting he might be afraid? He'd have to wait and see . . .

Actually, Studer would quite liked to have had another word with Frau Aeschbacher. What kind of a woman was she? She had a strange way of speaking. A foreigner? Where had a coarse fellow like Aeschbacher found such a refined wife. She wouldn't spend the night reading romantic novels, that was for sure. Perhaps she played the piano? Or the violin? His headache was back. But it would all be over soon. Actually, he could have asked for a uniform corporal from Bern to take Aeschbacher in. Then he could have crawled into bed straight away. Wouldn't it be better if he went home to his own bed. Hedy wasn't bad at nursing. Why bother with the hospital at all? The door opened.

"Shall we go, then?" asked Aeschbacher, as calmly as if they were going for a Sunday-afternoon drive.

Studer stood up. His mouth was dry. He had a funny hollow feeling in his stomach. It came from the fever, lack of food and alcohol on an empty stomach, he told himself. But the feeling refused to go away.

Out for a spin

If it hadn't been for his hands, those large, fat hands on the wheel which twitched every now and then to adjust the steering, he could have believed he was sitting next to a stone statue. Aeschbacher didn't move. His mouth was firmly shut, his eyes fixed straight ahead. The windscreen wipers swung to and fro, making a geometrical figure on the grimy windscreen which reminded Studer of school.

"Does your wife come from abroad?" he asked hesitantly, just to break the silence.

No reply. Studer stole a glance at Aeschbacher. He saw two large tears run down his blubbery cheeks and disappear into his moustache; two more followed, disappeared. Embarrassed, Studer looked the other way. Like so much in life, it looked both tragic and grotesque.

One hand left the steering wheel, felt in a pocket. A nose was blown.

"This bloody cold." The voice was hoarse. "She grew up in Vienna. Her parents were Swiss."

"And what does she think about all this?" Studer could have kicked himself. That was definitely not the thing to say. He'd made a mistake. Aeschbacher's eyes were suddenly on him, the look in them more malevolent even than the look he'd given him in the Bear, all those days ago. Studer could still see the single movement with which he fanned out his cards . . .

The voice was quite calm now. "You shouldn't have said that, sergeant."

The road ran along the lake, but there was hardly anything of it to be seen. There was the width of the road, then a low wall. Beyond the wall a large, moist expanse could just be made out, grey, grey, blurred, cold. The car was going slowly.

What time was it? Studer went to take out his watch. His thumb and forefinger were already in his waistcoat pocket when he heard an unknown voice (with no similarity at all to the voice of the announcer on Radio Bern) say, "Out! Get out! Otherwise . . ."

Studer's watch flew out of his waistcoat pocket, his right hand grasped the door handle, pushed it down, pulled it up (how the hell did this handle work?), he threw his whole weight against the door, it burst open, he shot out into the road, caught his foot on the bottom of the door frame, was dragged along a short way, his shoulder, his head hit something hard, a gigantic shadow loomed over him, disappeared . . . Then everything went black.

* * *

"No," a deep voice was saying, "you're not going to use the microscope just now." It was dark. Somewhere there was a green light. Studer desperately tried to remember where he had heard that voice.

"Picric acid . . ." Studer whispered. He heard a laugh.

"That blasted detective, never gives up, does he? Now, nurse, as I said, nikethamide every hour, transpulmine every three hours. Constitution of an ox, thank God. It's no joke when you've got two fractures, plus . . ."

That was all Studer heard. There had been a black curtain, surely, but now a red one descended on him, a roaring, bells ringing . . . The whisky was strong . . . It gave you a thirst. . . . What did the lake look like? A broad expanse, grey, grey, cold and moist . . .

Then the sun was back and a familiar sound. Studer listened. A click-click. What was it? He knew it so well, it was a noise that used to drive him crazy. What on earth was it? Of course! Knitting needles. He called out softly, "Hedy."

"Yes?"

A shadow between him and the sun.

"Hello," said Studer, blinking.

"*Salut,*" said Frau Studer, as if it were the most natural thing in the world.

"What's wrong with me?" Studer asked.

"Oh, nothing special. A temperature, pleurisy, a broken arm, a fractured collar-bone. You should be glad you're still alive."

She looked as if she was annoyed, but now and then her lips twitched.

"Oh, I am, I am," Studer replied and went back to sleep.

The third time he felt much better. The pain in his chest, the stabbing pain had gone. But his right arm felt heavy. Studer drank a cup of clear soup and went back to sleep.

The fourth time he woke up because there was a hell of a row going on outside his door. An irritating voice was demanding to be let in, another voice (wasn't that Dr. Neuenschwander?) got angry and swore. It was all so unbearably loud.

"Tell them to shut up," Studer whispered.

Not long after they did.

Then finally came the great awakening. It was morning, cool, the window must have just been opened. The room was small, the walls covered in green gloss paint. There were geraniums in bloom on the window-sill.

A fat nurse was sweeping the floor.

"Nurse," said Studer, and his voice was back to normal, "I'm hungry."

"Are you now?" was all the nurse said. Then she came across and bent over him. "Feeling better?"

"Where am I?" asked Studer, then started to laugh. That was the question the heroes were always asking in those novels by . . . by . . . what was she called, the old trout who kept on writing novels? Felicitas? That was it, Felicitas . . .

"Gerzenstein General Hospital," the nurse said. There was music coming from somewhere.

"What's that?" Studer asked.

"A concert, from the harbour in Hamburg," the nurse said.

"Gerzenstein and its wireless sets," Studer muttered. Then there was milk and rolls and butter and jam. Studer felt like a Brissago, but when he said so out loud he got a sharp response from the nurse.

Then came an afternoon when he was alone in his room. His wife had gone back to Bern, promising to return at the end of the week to take him home.

The nurse came in and said a lady (she said "lady") wanted to speak to the sergeant. Studer nodded.

The lady had white hair, white as . . . as lilac.

Studer knew that Aeschbacher had drowned in the lake. An accident, they'd said. Studer had nodded.

The lady sat down by Studer's bed. The nurse went out. The lady remained silent.

"Bonjour, madame," Studer said in a feeble attempt at levity. The lady nodded.

Silence. A bumble-bee buzzed round the room. It must be the end of June.

"It was my fault," said Studer. "I asked him about you, and he started to cry. The tears were running down his cheeks. Yes. And then I asked him what you thought, you know, about the whole business. He gave me a warning. I just had time to jump out of the car. I presume he just went straight . . . Better that way, don't you think?"

"Yes," the lady said. She didn't cry. She had put her hand on Studer's arm. It was light as a feather.

"I won't say anything, madame," Studer said in a soft voice.

"Thank you, Herr Studer."

That was all.

And once Sonja Witschi came. To thank him. The insurance had not been paid out. The examining magistrate had summoned all three of them, Sonja, her mother and Armin. It had been decided not to charge them with attempted fraud. The authorities had been glad simply to be able to regard the Witschi case as closed.

How was Schlumpf, Studer wanted to know.

"Fine," said Sonja, blushing, freckles on the bridge of her nose, her temples.

"Armin's going to get married soon too," she added. "Mother's still got the station kiosk."

Finally the examining magistrate came. This time the silk shirt he was wearing was cream. He still had his signet ring.

"I came once before, Herr Studer," he said. "But the doctor was so offensive. I continue to be amazed at the lack of manners among men who've had a university education — especially doctors."

That was the way things were, Studer replied. He had his hands clasped on the bedspread and was twiddling his thumbs.

196

"Why were you in the car with Aeschbacher, Herr Studer? Had you discovered something important? At the time you dropped such strange hints. Did Witschi actually commit suicide, or was it murder after all? Did the late mayor give you some information? Something important? Information he wanted to give me too? You're not saying anything, Studer. What did Aeschbacher tell you that sent you hurrying like that with him to Thun?"

Studer stared at the ceiling and was silent for a while. Then he said, in a toneless voice, "Nothing special . . ."

Glauser on Glauser

You want facts? Right then: Born Vienna, 1896, Austrian mother and Swiss father. Grandfather on my father's side a gold-digger in California *(sans blague)*, on my mother's side a senior civil servant (fantastic combination, don't you think?). Primary school, three years high school in Vienna. Then three years at the Glarisegg Reform School. Then three years at the Collège de Genève. Thrown out shortly before taking the school-leaving examinations . . . took them in Zurich. Then Dadaism. My father wanted to have me locked away and placed under a legal guardian. Ran away to Geneva . . . detained in Münsingen for a year (1919). Escaped from there. One year in Ascona. Arrested for morphine. Sent back. Three months in Burghölzli (for a second opinion, because Geneva had declared me schizophrenic). 1921–23 Foreign Legion. Then Paris, washer-up. Belgium, coalmines. Later hospital orderly in Charleroi. Morphine again. Imprisoned in Belgium. Deported to Switzerland. Ordered to do one year in Witzwil. Afterwards one year labourer in a tree nursery. Analysis (one year) . . . To Basel as a gardener, then Wintherthur. During that time (1928/29) wrote my Foreign Legion novel, '30/'31 one-year course at the Oeschberg tree nursery. July '31 follow-up analysis. January '32 to July '32, Paris as a "freelance writer" (as the saying goes). Went to visit my father in Mannheim. Arrested there for forged prescriptions. Deported to Switzerland. Imprisoned from July '32-May '36. *Et puis voilà. Ce n'est pas très beau . . .*

Letter to Joseph Halperin, 15 June 1937

Praise for Glauser

"From bitter experience Glauser has painted a portrait of Switzerland you will never see in a travel brochure"
Frankfurter Allgemeine Zeitung

"A magician of atmosphere, the best of the George Simenon school"
Neue Zürcher Zeitung

"At the end of his life Glauser had ambitious plans for Sergeant Studer, but the five novels he left us are sufficient to guarantee his hero the place he deserves in the history of crime fiction"
Le Monde

"Like Maigret, Studer begins by immersing himself in the milieu of his suspects. He becomes part of it"
Süddeutsche Zeitung

"Elegant and crystal-clear writing"
Le Monde

"Glauser has elevated his material to an exquisite artistic level, a master of psychological analysis, a warm, sensitive and wonderfully observant writer"
Der Bund

"Perfect characterization, brilliant portrayal of humour and irony against the dark, brooding background of small-town life"
Nationalzeitung Basel

"Friedrich Glauser is a remarkable discovery. An ability to translate an erratic, obsessive life into language that seduces by its intimacy. A reflection of his suffering and compassion"
Bayerische Rundfunk, Munich

BITTER LEMON PRESS
LONDON

Bringing you the best literary crime and *romans noirs* from Europe, Africa and Latin America.

Thumbprint   *Friedrich Glauser*

A classic of European crime writing. Glauser, the Swiss Simenon, introduces Sergeant Studer, the hero of five novels.

January 2004   ISBN 1–904738–00–1   £8.99 pb

Holy Smoke   *Tonino Benacquista*

A story of wine, miracles, the mafia and the Vatican. Darkly comic writing by a best-selling author.

January 2004   ISBN 1–904738–01–X   £8.99 pb

The Russian Passenger   *Günter Ohnemus*

An offbeat crime story involving the Russian mafia but also a novel of desperate love and insight into the cruel history that binds Russia and Germany.

March 2004   ISBN 1–904738–02–8   £9.99 pb

Tequila Blue   *Rolo Diez*

A police detective with a wife, a mistress and a string of whores. This being Mexico, he resorts to arms dealing, extortion and money laundering to finance the pursuit of justice.

May 2004   ISBN 1–904738–04–4   £8.99 pb

Goat Song   *Chantal Pelletier*

A double murder at the Moulin Rouge. Dealers, crack addicts and girls dreaming of glory who end up in porn videos.

July 2004   ISBN 1–904738–03–6   £8.99 pb

The Snowman   *Jörg Fauser*

Found: two kilos of Peruvian flake, the best cocaine in the world. Money for nothing. A fast-paced crime novel set in Malta, Munich and Ostend.

September 2004   ISBN 1–904738–05–2   £8.99 pb

www.bitterlemonpress.com